Everybody Knows

A SMALL-TOWN ROMANCE

HONEYBEE HOLLOW

ARIELLA TALIX

There is a comfortable feeling in small towns. It is salubrious.
—Andie MacDowell

Content Warning

1. Violence
2. Explicit sex
3. Bad grammar used intentionally for authenticity

CHAPTER

One

BLAKE

THERE MUST BE SOMETHING WRONG WITH ME.

This morning, I was out of coffee, so I dropped in at Juni's place, Hot Stuff. It's the local coffeehouse/bakery here in Honeybee Hollow. Juni seemed a little overly happy to see me and introduced me to her new employee Sloane Morgan. Apparently, the last helper took off suddenly and left Juni in the lurch. Anyway, this new girl, I mean woman—she may look young, but *damn* she's all woman—is spectacular. I intended to take a regular coffee in a to-go cup and get to work since I'd already had breakfast, but suddenly I was *starved* for a cinnamon roll. I even ordered a large coffee just so I could have an excuse to sit around longer.

Now I'm sitting here in the same room as this vision, trying my damnedest not to stare.

This is so not me.

Fortunately, it's still early, and Juni's two life partners, Jack and Asher, are lingering too. They're great guys, and usually I enjoy talking to them, but today I am struggling to listen and look semi-lucid as they tell me all about their new house.

I can't pay attention or keep my eyes off this amazing creature. She's soft-spoken as far as I can tell—I mean she said it was nice to meet me and asked me for my order politely, but now I hope I'm not a moony-eyed goofball.

Juni likes to wear short shorts when it's warm enough, and apparently, she's told her new employee to do the same—even though it's March and still a little nippy. So Sloane is bending over wiping away the small spills and crumbs from a nearby table, and I'm trying to keep my tongue in my mouth. Those shapely legs of hers! She has big brown eyes and medium-length, silky mahogany hair currently pulled back into a low ponytail. I suddenly get the urge to wrap that shiny hank of hair in my fist while I...

"Blake? Yo, Deputy Ogden," Jack says with a chuckle.

"Huh?" I respond brilliantly as my gaze snaps to Jack's face. My dumb voice even cracks. What am I, twelve? I resist the urge to check my chin for drool.

"We just asked if you'd be able to come to our party at the house this Saturday night. You don't have to work, do you?"

"Juni told us to be sure to ask you," Asher adds in his rumbling voice. Why do his eyes look like he's trying to hold in a laugh? Do I have frosting on my face? I swipe a napkin across my mouth just in case.

I drag my attention back to the conversation at the table and answer, "No, I don't have to work. Thanks, guys, that would be great. Can I bring something?"

"Oh, maybe some beer or whatever you like to drink. We have most of it covered," Jack tells me. "And you can certainly bring a date." His eyes dart to Sloane so briefly I almost miss it.

I wonder what Sloane likes to drink. Should I ask her? What is happening to me? I haven't been interested in a woman ever since… don't go there. Sure, there have been a few hookups. I mean, I'm no monk—even though I pretend to be around here. But I haven't paid much attention to anyone in Honeybee Hollow. Since I'm the chief deputy sheriff, I generally satisfy my needs in neighboring towns instead of giving a local lady the wrong idea. And I always make it clear I'm only there for the sex and not a relationship. It's surprising to me how many women are happy with that.

Sloane finishes her cleanup job, and I watch her like a hawk as she makes her way back around the counter. Juni hands her a coffee carafe and says something I can't hear in a low voice. Juni's eyes dart to me, and she grins when she sees they have my attention. She gives me a wink and turns around as Sloane approaches the table.

"Can I top you off, gentlemen?" she asks. How does she make that sound so sexy?

I detect a trace of a Yankee accent. She's not southern, that's for sure. Maybe she's from New York or New Jersey. What's she doing in these parts? If I weren't so tongue-tied, I'd ask her. But all I manage is a choked out, "Uh… sure. Thanks." If I keep chugging coffee like this, I'm going to be wired for the rest of the day. I know I need to get to the office pretty soon, but my ass is glued to this seat, and I can't move.

I can't help wondering when Juni started handing out free refills. Oh well, maybe it's because I'm sitting with her guys.

As soon as Sloane refills my coffee, Asher and Jack jump up and announce they have to get to work. For Asher, that means the corporate camp he manages. For Jack, the art gallery around the corner. Asher squeezes my shoulder, then they both kiss Juni goodbye and whisper some things to her that make her eyes light up. As they exit the door, they kiss each other goodbye too. They never cease to amaze me with their open affection. It must be nice to feel so free and not give a hoot about anything other folks might think about them.

I'm about to take my coffee and hit the road too, but Sloane approaches my table again and says, "Um, sorry if I'm intruding. For some reason Juni says I'm due to take a break for a few minutes… she told me I should come talk to you. But if that bothers you, I'll just go outside for a bit."

"*No*," I choke out. "I mean, please have a seat." I stare at her a second too long and blurt out, "When did you start working for Juni?"

She gives me a tiny smile and says, "This morning. I just met her yesterday."

"Welcome to Honeybee Hollow then, Sloane. Where are you from? Not Kentucky, if I could venture a guess."

Her cheeks go a little pink, and she mumbles, "Oh, uh, no. I'm from… up north."

Well, that narrows it down to about fifteen possible states… and Canada. I'm about to politely ask her to be more specific when my phone rings. "Excuse me," I tell her.

"Blake, where the hell are you? Something's wrong with Sheriff Hansen! I've called the EMTs, and they're on their way, but you need to get here *now*!" Birdie Bianchi, our dispatch operator, almost screams at me from the phone.

"This is bad," I mutter as I stand and run for the door. I turn around and apologize, "Sorry, emergency!" And I'm outta there in a dead run. I can't imagine what's going on.

CHAPTER
Two

Sloane

"That was unfortunate," Juni tells me as I watch the rapidly retreating form of the best-looking man I've seen in years—or maybe ever. It's a little strange, feeling attracted to someone in a police uniform. Or maybe he's a sheriff. I'm not even sure what they have in this town—only that they called him "Deputy." All I can be sure of is that the Honeybee Hollow men are spectacular, and the women are pretty and friendly.

Yesterday, I followed the road signs leading to "The Best Small Town in America" and blew into Honeybee Hollow. I had a suitcase of clothes and a large, beat-up gym bag locked in the trunk of my cute little white Honda, and it took me less than ten minutes to find not only a job but a place to live from the coolest employer/landlord ever. Juniper Barry owns Hot

Stuff, and she had a Help Wanted sign in the window and a vacant, furnished apartment upstairs. She used to live there, but she left so she could move in with her *two* boyfriends. Whew, go Juni! Her previous employee lived up there for a couple of months after Juni moved, but she vacated it a few days ago when she left town in a rush.

As soon as I walked through the door of Hot Stuff, I was in love. The smell of coffee and baked goods wrapped around me like a fluffy blanket. Juni is gorgeous with long, wavy blonde hair and a killer smile as inviting as the aromas surrounding her. The furnishings are brightly colored and comfy-looking, and one wall has a stunning mural on it that depicts smiling people all gathered over coffee and pastries. It reminds me of a Renoir painting, only everyone is in modern clothing. I noticed a signature in the corner that says "Skyler," and I wonder who that is. Skyler is quite an artist—I can tell you that.

When Juni found out that I know how to make change, run a credit card reader, brew coffee, and follow a recipe, she asked me what size t-shirt I wear.

"Medium."

Juni eyed me carefully and handed me two *small* Hot Stuff t-shirts with deeply scooped necklines. "You have great tits," she said matter-of-factly. "These will show them off and get you better tips." She grinned and shook my hand. I was hired. The shirts are actually kinda cute, but a little suggestive because they have silkscreened muffins positioned right over my boobs with a steaming cup of coffee between them. Maybe that's why that cute deputy kept staring at me so hard. Juni also recommended short skirts or shorts unless it's snowing. She promised the ovens keep this place pretty toasty in most weather, and the more skin that shows, the better. It feels like working at an upscale Hooters—without the booze and wings.

This is the perfect job for me since I have experience as a barista. It's low stress, I have late afternoons and evenings free, and by working, I'll blend into the community better than if I did nothing but spend money. I'll be able to meet people more easily than if I were all on my own.

So I'm sitting here woolgathering about Deputy McHottie when I realize Juni is still talking to me. "If he doesn't get in touch with you about being his date, you'll just have to come out to the party on your own. I'm telling you, though, Sloane, that man needs a girlfriend. He's wasting his youth being single. And I don't mean that he's catting around having a fun time being single—I mean he's alone all the time. He doesn't even have a dog. It's a crime against all that is natural to waste his great looks and brains on that stupid job he has. He needs a distraction before he turns into a grumpy old man."

"What's wrong with his job?"

"He's the deputy sheriff and works with a couple other guys under a doddering old fool who thinks littering is the crime of the century. If anything of substance actually happened in this town, I doubt the sheriff would recognize it unless it bit him on the butt. I honestly cannot imagine what kind of emergency got Blake so worked up that he ran out of here like he did. It's not the kind of thing that happens in our sleepy little town."

I inwardly give a relieved sigh. I love the idea of no crime and a quiet life. This town seems perfect for me to decompress. I just hope I don't get bored after what I'm used to.

"Thanks, Juni. I'm not really ready to be in a relationship, but I'd love to go to a party where I can meet some of your friends. This town seems like a great place to live."

"It's sure been good for me," she says, eyeing me speculatively. "We have one good friend who grew up here, but several of the people around our age moved here because of the business opportunities and the culture. You'll see how terrific it is as you get to know the residents. Anyway, I need to go grab some stuff out of the oven in a minute, so take over the counter, please. It's about to get busy in here, judging by the time. Our second wave of morning people are due any minute."

Just then, an ambulance zooms past the coffeehouse with lights flashing and siren wailing. "Oh no." I turn to Juni, who looks as worried as I feel. "What do you think happened?"

"Beats me, but I bet it has to do with why Blake ran out of here. Maybe there was a car accident." She goes to the window and cranes her neck. "One thing's for sure. We'll know as soon as this place fills up. Small-town news travels like lightning. Everybody knows everyone else's business… or they think they do."

Sure enough, three middle-aged ladies come fluttering in all red-faced and chattering like magpies. "Juni! Did you hear?" one of them asks. "They're taking Sheriff Hansen out of his office on a stretcher!"

"We don't know," exclaims another who is clutching her large purse to her chest, "whether he had a medical emergency or he was attacked! This is so awful."

"Who would attack Sheriff Hansen?" Juni asks. "He's an old man who plays computer solitaire at his desk all day trying to make himself look busy."

"Well, I wouldn't know, but with all of the new people who keep moving into town, maybe one of them is a *criminal* or something." She looks in the pastry case and adds, "Be a dear, would you, and box up half a dozen of your wonderful cranberry orange muffins?"

Juni gasps. She spins around looking stricken. "My muffins are going to burn! Sloane, please take care of the ladies." And she darts away. I don't smell any smoke, so hopefully she remembered in time.

Each of the three ladies takes off with a box of pastries, and other people start pouring through the door, just as Juni predicted. For the next two hours, we're ridiculously busy and have very little time to do anything other than sell, serve, and straighten up the tables. The tip jar is practically overflowing, and everyone is extremely friendly to me. The private snippets of conversation we hear are all nosy speculation about the sheriff, but no one really knows anything. The stories range from "Someone in the holding cell pulled a knife on Sheriff Hansen" to "He dropped dead of a heart attack." Juni pronounces the first one ridiculous, and I sure hope for the old man's sake it's not the second.

When things finally settle down, and I have a chance to take a breath and sit down for a moment with a bottle of water, a gorgeous young woman and two incredibly hot guys come in. The woman is obviously pregnant with an adorable baby bump. They're all smiles, and she says, "Hi. You must be Sloane. Juni told me you'd be here. I'm Juni's bestie Brooke, and this is my husband Levi," She gestures to the dark-haired guy, "and our boyfriend Skyler." She indicates the blond man splattered with a little paint, and I immediately remember the signature on the mural. Interesting. She spelled their relationship out in no uncertain terms, didn't she? "Juni has a special order ready for us."

Juni apparently heard them come in and pops out of the kitchen with a large bag in her hands. "Hi, guys." She gasps, "*Wow*, Brooke. You're even bigger than you were a few days ago. What do you have growing in there?" She comes around the counter to get a better look.

Brooke laughs and rubs her belly. "A future linebacker, no doubt." She grins as the guy she called Levi nuzzles her neck and rubs her belly too. I get goosebumps at the devotion in his eyes.

Juni turns to me and announces, "Don't ever charge any of them for their orders. We have a barter system going because of Skyler's amazing artwork." While she's busy telling me this, Skyler quietly stuffs a fifty into the tip jar behind her. Apparently, he's not all that concerned with bartering.

"Oh, okay." I look at Skyler, who has stepped back beside Brooke with a satisfied look on his face. "Your painting is incredibly beautiful."

"Thanks," he tells me. "Are you going to join us all at the party this weekend, Sloane?" Evidently, he doesn't need anyone gushing over his talents, but he does look pleased.

"Oh, yes, definitely. I'm anxious to meet people."

"Great," Brooke exclaims. "Juni and I want to make sure you meet…"

Juni laughs and interrupts, "Blake has already been in for coffee, and he couldn't take his eyes off Sloane this morning. We're off to a great start." Whatever that means. I feel like the victim of a conspiracy as Juni winks at Brooke—who looks happy.

Levi steps back and asks, "Are you two scheming?"

"We're just trying to help out our friends," Brooke answers.

"Maybe they can take care of themselves."

Juni pipes up, "I'm sure Sloane can, but Deputy Blake needs some assistance. The man is going to get old and die alone the way he's going."

"He's only a couple of years older than me," Levi says with a mock frown.

"And you're all hitched up tighter than a drum, my dear husband. There's no comparison."

He laughs at her and throws up his hands. "I just hope you don't get into trouble. I think our buddy Blake may have his reasons."

This sounds ominous to me, but before I have the chance to ask Levi what he means, a big group of people file in with coffee and pastry orders, and I need to take care of them. By the time I'm done, Levi, Skyler, and Brooke have gone. They did wave and say they were looking forward to seeing me later. They seem so nice and look so happy. I hope everyone I meet is this nice.

We'll see.

CHAPTER
Three

BLAKE

OH NO. AS SOON AS I ENTER THE SHERIFF'S OFFICE, I CAN SEE that the situation is grim. Sheriff Hansen is lying on the floor next to his desk, and our dispatcher is holding his hand. He looks unresponsive. I kneel at his side to check for breathing and a pulse. His breathing is shallow, and his pulse is weak. His color isn't good, and his chin is bleeding.

"Tell me what happened, Birdie."

"He was standing by his desk when he made kind of a funny noise, and just as I looked over at him, he grabbed his head and toppled over, smacking his face on his desk. He can't talk and doesn't seem to hear me at all. I called for an ambulance, and then I called you. Oh, I can hear them coming now." Sure enough, there is a wailing siren that's getting closer.

"Was he making any jerky movements or clenching his teeth?"

"I don't really know. I don't think so," she says as her eyes fill with tears.

"It sounds like he might have had a stroke. Not a seizure or a heart attack, but we'll let the medical people figure this out." I look for signs that one side of his face is drooping, but he's pretty symmetrical to me. I can't tell if one side of his body is weak because he's not moving at all. "Sheriff? Can you hear me?" Nothing. Not even an eyelid flicker.

Soon the EMT guys are rushing in with a gurney and some oxygen. They get him loaded up in seconds and tell us they're heading straight to the emergency room. I'm not sure whether to leave to join them or man the office, but then it hits me that I need to call his wife and let her know.

She's a wreck by the time I'm done speaking to her, and I'm just about ready to go pick her up myself when one of the other officers shows up. I send him to get her. I figure since I'm actually chief deputy—even though no one bothers to call me that—the office is now under my command.

I make my way to my desk and look through last night's records to see if anything requires attention. Thank heaven there isn't much, so I'm about to go make a pot of coffee for the other guys (I've had enough) when the mayor comes barging in all puffed up with authority. Honestly, he's a great guy, but he does love a crisis.

"Blake! Tell me what happened. I heard they took Sheriff Hansen outta here in an ambulance." He booms at me like he's addressing a crowd of three hundred, even though it's only me and Birdie. She does lots of odd jobs around the office because there is only a small amount of actual dispatching that needs to be done on most days. Right now, she's cleaning up Sheriff Hansen's desk and straightening the loose papers he pulled onto the floor when he fell.

She looks terribly shaken, so I guess she needs to keep busy. Birdie's been at this job for years and years and probably knows everything that's gone on in this town forever.

I do my best to fill in Mayor Stevens. He's a good man, but people say he's no match for our former mayor, Tanner Lassiter, who went on to become governor. Still, they were buddies back when he served on the town counsel under Lassiter and seems to have many of the same values. I've never had cause to criticize the man.

He listens to me carefully and then says, "Blake, as mayor of this fine town, and given your seniority in the sheriff's office, it is my duty to swear you in as the new sheriff—effective immediately. It's painfully obvious that Sheriff Hansen is not fit for duty, and we can't be without senior law enforcement running this office at all times. Also, I know that he was on the brink of retirement because I'd discussed it with him just recently. Normally, we'd have a nice public ceremony for you and give you your new badge, but I don't want to take the time. If you'd like, we can head over to the courthouse and meet in Judge Jenkins's chambers. If we do it there, it'll seem more official, plus he called me just as I was heading over here and recommended it. I think he likes the idea of being part of something important like this."

"Um…" I'm having a hard time wrapping my head around this happening so suddenly. "I guess that would be alright."

"Fine, fine. That will give me a chance to pick up a copy of the oath of office for you back at my office. I'll meet you at the courthouse in ten minutes. That okay with you?" He starts for the door, then turns to ask, "Is there anyone you'd like to have join us? Girlfriend? Best friend? That might make it more meaningful to you, but time's a-wastin', so make your call right now if you want to round up anyone."

Incongruously, my mind instantly falls on Sloane. How crazy is that? I just met the woman less than an hour ago, and I've barely spoken to her. "Oh, uh… no, it's fine. I'll just head on over in a couple of minutes. Thank you, Mayor." What is wrong with me? I must have friends in this town, but no one else comes to mind.

Before he leaves, Mayor Stevens barks, "Birdie, please alert the town paper, if you will. Let 'em know we have a new sheriff in town." He waves at us and marches out the door as she stares at him.

The ceremony takes all of five minutes, and it's about as exciting as a glass of lukewarm milk. The only thing that kept it from being next to nothing is that a photographer from the paper came bustling in to take a few shots just as we were getting started.

I raise my hand and promise to do the job with honesty, integrity, and to the best of my ability. I get back slaps from the mayor and the judge and then head out. Before I make it through the door, Mayor Stevens stops me saying, "We'll special order you that new badge, so you ought to have it in a couple of days." I nod my thanks.

I don't even have any family I can call to tell about my promotion. Is this how it feels when they cheer, "Long live the king!" for you when your father—the real king—suddenly dies and you feel like an impostor with the new job. *Oh stop it, I tell myself. You're the furthest thing from royalty there is. You're just a simple lawman in a little bitty town in rural Kentucky.* It sure feels significant at the moment though. Although he's a good man, I was never all that crazy about Sheriff Hansen and thought he made mountains out of mole-hills—probably because he was bored. But I sure thought he'd have the chance to retire on his own terms. I feel a little like a pretender suddenly.

I make my way over to the hospital to check on Sheriff

Hansen. The news is grim. He's had a cerebral aneurysm, so now he's on life support, and he's completely unresponsive. His poor wife is a mess, but her neighbors and friends from their church—in typical Honeybee Hollow fashion—have already heard the news and are surrounding her with comfort and love. I give her what kind words I can muster up and promise to keep them both in my prayers. She thanks me and asks, "What about the office? What will happen now?"

I'm almost embarrassed to tell her, "Mayor Stevens just swore me in as the new sheriff. I'll pack up all of your husband's belongings and drop them by your house whenever it's convenient for you."

A tear streaks down her cheek that she wipes away with a tissue. This must be so hard on her. Hansen's been the sheriff here for years and years. He never ran opposed, so the job has been automatic, and I understand how this is a sudden change she'll have to deal with along with the uncertainty of her husband's health. She gives me a wobbly smile and says, "Congratulations on your promotion, Blake. I'm sure you'll do a fine job. My husband always had the nicest things to say about you."

"Thank you, ma'am." Now I feel even worse considering I never said anything particularly nice about him. At least I didn't badmouth him… I don't think. Well… not too much, anyway. Okay, honestly, the guy was not fit to be the sheriff, and he was pretty bad at it.

I head back to the office and begin the process of moving

ex-Sheriff Hansen out and me into my new private office. It's weird to think of it as mine now. I'm relieved we don't have anyone in lockup at the moment because my head is too full of uncertainty to be able to cope with anything like that right now. It makes me sad to fill a box with family photos and personal mementos for him. It's like his life is suddenly reduced to the contents of that box, so I pack everything carefully, giving it the respect it deserves.

One thing occurs to me. I'll be making more money now. The salary isn't huge, but it's significantly more than I've been making. Maybe I can do… something. I don't even know what. My life has always consisted of hardship and hard work, so luxury has never been in the cards. I have a mortgage on an old house on the edge of town that I bought for next to nothing and spent lots of sweat equity fixing up from its decrepit state into something that makes me proud. Maybe I'll pay off the mortgage. That sounds responsible.

I'm just about done getting myself moved in when I look up to see Juni and Sloane sauntering in with a bag of something that smells wonderful. Juni has a huge grin, but Sloane looks a bit more hesitant. "We just closed and thought you might like some lunch after your big day. Have you eaten yet?" Juni asks. "If you did eat, you can always have this for your supper."

"Uh, hi. Um… no I haven't eaten. So much has happened, I sort of lost track of time." Just then, my stomach lets out a huge rumble—probably from the delicious smell of whatever she picked up from the local deli.

"Well, this is our way of saying congratulations on your promotion," Juni announces, beaming at me. "The news is all over town."

"Uh, yeah, congratulations, Sher… uh… Blake," Sloane adds with an unsure smile. She looks so cute and appealing to me, I know I'm fucked. I also see that she's wisely traded in her skimpy shorts for a pair of skinny jeans more suited to walking around outside in this weather. I don't know if my mouth is watering because of the food or the sight of her.

"Wow, thanks, ladies. This is really nice of you." I take a peek into the bag, and the delicious aroma knocks me over.

Juni gets a rather theatrical look on her face and announces, "Oops! I forgot I was supposed to go meet Jack at his gallery to help him with something. I need to run, but you stay, Sloane. Keep Blake company while he has lunch." She doesn't even wait for an answer and rushes out the door calling over her shoulder, "See you both tomorrow! Blake, you might want to drive Sloane out to our place since she doesn't know the way." And she's gone.

Sloane's face turns an adorable shade of pink as she rolls her eyes. "Sorry. Juni's great, but she's not subtle, I've learned."

"No need to apologize. Would you like to share some of this with me? It looks like an awful lot of food. Have you eaten?"

"I haven't, but I don't want to eat your lunch…" she starts to protest until I pull out two wrapped gyros and a couple of side dishes. Laughing, she says, "Oh Juni. Like I said, she's not subtle. She went out and got this while I was cleaning up at Hot Stuff. I'd love to join you unless you need the second one for dinner or something."

"Have a seat. I'll just go grab a couple of waters from the fridge. I need a break, and I'd love to have your company." I head out of the office to the small kitchenette and root around until I find two bottles of water and a couple paper plates. It looks like the fridge could use some attention too. Some of this stuff must have been in there for weeks. A problem for another time.

As we settle in and start to enjoy our lunch, I have to ask Sloane, "How did you happen to come to Honeybee Hollow? Have you ever been here before, or do you know someone here?"

She smiles shyly at me and sets down her gyros. "Neither. I'm sure you'll think this sounds silly, but when I was pretty little, my parents dragged me to a beach party in Southampton. Once we got there, they sort of ignored me so my dad could schmooze. I didn't know any of the kids—who were also ignoring me—so I wandered around and saw two young men who were deep in conversation. I thought they were absolutely beautiful and made up a story in my head about how they were fairytale princes." She looks down and shakes her head. "I know, goofy kid." I don't answer that as she continues, "So I eavesdropped on them hoping they'd say something about a princess or a dragon, but I got frustrated when I couldn't hear them well. So I marched up to them, and I think I asked them something dumb like whether they lived in a castle. Of course, they just laughed, but they were polite. One of them started to tell me he didn't live in a castle, but he did come from this wonderful, magical town called Honeybee Hollow in Kentucky. He made it sound like the best place to live. He also had an exotic—to my little ears—southern accent that I loved. And he told me that he planned to become mayor of that perfect little town, and when I grew up, I ought to come and see the place."

At this point I start to laugh, and Sloane looks at me with an embarrassed expression. "I'm not laughing at you, Sloane. That must have been Tanner Lassiter and the billionaire who became his campaign manager when he ran for governor. They were college friends, I understand—Princeton, if I have it right. He did become mayor and then governor, but you must have been awfully young to be wandering around by yourself."

"Eh. My parents didn't pay much attention to me until I got older, so I was used to it. Besides, the partygoers were just a bunch of people my dad wanted to impress. But… I wasn't worth as much to them back then." Noticing my quick frown, she turns pink again and takes a big gulp of water like she's said too much. "Anyway, I forgot all about that day until recently when I ran across a piece of paper stuffed in a drawer of my childhood bedroom. I'd written 'Honeybee Hollow' on it, surrounded by a heart, and the memory of that party came back to me. A short time later, I… um… wanted a change of scenery, so I found it on Google Maps and headed south. I've only been here for a couple of days, but I have to say, as towns go, it seems pretty special, and the people sure are friendly." She gives me a speculative look and asks, "How about you? Were you lucky enough to grow up here?"

I don't miss that she told me all about how she'd heard about Honeybee Hollow but not a word about why she actually ended up here in need of a change of scenery. And then she abruptly diverted the attention onto me instead of elaborating. Interesting. I let out a long breath and hope I don't have to go into too much detail about my background. "No. I grew up in Harlan County but not here. I came here when they had an opening for a deputy position in the sheriff's office. It is nice, isn't it?" We can both be evasive, my beautiful Sloane.

The rest of our conversation is surface level and impersonal, but I don't want to scare her off, so I go with it. I tell her about the local shops, restaurants, and bars of interest to most people. I also tell her about the hat factory Tanner's sister owns and suggest she take the tour, although I don't offer to take her on it. "It's a lot more interesting than it sounds," I promise. All too soon, Birdie lets me know there's been a three-car wreck just north of town, and I have to scoot.

"Thanks again for bringing lunch, Sloane. I hope to see you tomorrow. Oh, um… do you need a ride?" Out of habit, I don't want to make it sound like a date, and I immediately mentally kick myself in the ass. Her happy, eager expression disappears, and she looks embarrassed.

"No, thanks anyway. I'll make my way out to their place. I'm sure I can get directions from someone. I'll just clean up this mess and get out of here."

"Okay. It's probably a good idea for you to go alone. You're a nice girl, but I'm not… uh…" Did I just say that out loud? Now I feel like a total asshole, and I really do need to leave, so I say, "I'll get the trash later. Don't worry." As I stride toward the door, I see that she's not paying any attention to me. I'm such a dumbass. Still… I don't see anything good coming from leading her on. Sure, she's gorgeous and I'm intrigued, but I made myself a promise three years ago to stay out of involvements. I've heard enough times that I make a terrible boyfriend.

At the same time, I can't help but wonder…

CHAPTER
Four

SLOANE

WOW. HE'S HANDSOME, BUT HE CERTAINLY HAS A COLD switch he can turn on quickly. I thought we were getting along pretty famously until he gave me the bum's rush. If he needed to work, he could have just done it—instead, he made sure I was clear on his disinterest. *"Oh, um, do you need a ride?"* It was painful.

I don't know why I'm complaining even to myself because I'm certainly not in any position to be looking for a boyfriend. And I like this town well enough so far, but would I feel claustrophobic here? It's pretty darn small. And their claim to fame is a *hat factory*? How odd. Still… the residents I've met don't act like hicks or country bumpkins.

They seem nice and sincere, actually—if not a little (a lot) gossipy.

When I finish cleaning up Blake's desk—whether he wanted me to or not—I introduce myself to the woman he called Birdie and ask if there's a grocery store nearby. I need to take something to the party tomorrow, and I also need a few things for my apartment. Once I get directions from her and thank her, I'm about to head out when she says out of the blue, "Give him time, honey. He's a nice boy. He'll come around."

The only reply I can think of is, "Uh… okay," because I'm so eloquent. I'm not even sure what she means.

I head back to my apartment with the plan to make up a list of what I think I'll need for the next few days. On the short walk back, several people stop me to say hi and welcome me to town. Everybody has apparently already heard that I'm working at Hot Stuff for Juni, but also my t-shirt does a good job of advertising that. The friendliness is so foreign to me, as is the stopping and chatting with strangers. I guess there are worse things.

Finally, with my list in hand, I head over by car to the Piggly Wiggly. I'm afraid I'll have too much to carry home if I walk. Again, in the store, I'm greeted by shoppers, some of whom call me by name. I've changed my shirt, so it's obvious a new face is a fresh sight. I guess the semi-full shopping cart differentiates me from a day tourist. When I finally step into the checkout line, I feel a warm presence at my back, and a funny zing goes through me, so I turn around and almost face-plant into the broad, hard chest of none other than Sheriff Blake.

He's eyeing me with his electric blue eyes boring into me intently. He's changed out of his uniform and into a pair of well-worn jeans and a gray Henley with the sleeves shoved up. His lean muscles are beautifully on display. Yum. He has a sack of coffee in his hand that he places on the conveyor belt.

"Sloane." His voice is quiet and low.

"Sheriff." I sound like a stuffy schoolmarm as I fight not to sniff and stick my nose in the air.

"It's *Blake*, Sloane," he grumbles. "I saw you here and wanted to apologize for my quick exit. I'm sorry I was rude."

"You were working, and I was intruding on your office hours. No offense taken."

"You were being nice, and I acted like a jerk."

Wow, this guy gives me whiplash. "Don't worry about it. I got your message loud and clear." I turn to pay my bill to the cashier. It takes a bit of time because I'm using cash and need to count out the right amount. It would be so much easier if I had a debit card. I make myself a note to take care of that soon. I hate using cash, and in my present situation that is so ironic.

I start to wheel my bags away in my cart, but a large, warm hand gently wraps around my arm. I turn quickly and don't miss the amused look on the cashier's face as she hands him his receipt. Immediately, I'm positive that more town gossip is being born right here, right now, and we're going to be at the center of it.

"Please don't run off. I wanted to ask if I could possibly take you out for a beer or a glass of wine. I'm off duty now, and I thought we could continue our conversation." I have to admit, the guy looks sincere. How long will this last?

"I have some stuff that needs refrigerating, but after I take care of that, I suppose maybe I could." Why am I agreeing?

"Terrific. I can meet you at your place, help you get all of this stuff upstairs, and then we can hit The Hive. If we get hungry, they have killer nachos. It's too early for live music, but when they have it, it's great."

Hungry? We just ate huge gyros for a late lunch. "I um, well… fine. I guess that would be okay. I mean it's nice of you." What do I mean? "I'll see you in a couple of minutes. You obviously know where I live." Inwardly, I cringe and wonder if the gossips will take that to mean he's *been* to my place already. I want to clarify that it's above Hot Stuff, and he knows I work there, but I keep my mouth shut. Instead of leaving, however, he follows me to my car and helps me put the bags into my trunk. You can't fault his manners at least.

ONCE WE'RE ALL DONE LUGGING MY GROCERIES UPSTAIRS TO the little kitchenette, he looks around curiously. "It's nice up here," he observes. "Small, but nice." It's really just one big room where the bed, sitting, and cooking areas all blend into one. It has a high ceiling and big windows, though, so it doesn't feel cramped. And it always smells like coffee and baked goods.

"Thanks. Excuse me a minute. I'll be right back. Make yourself comfortable." I leave him standing next to the little kitchen table and hurry into the bathroom. I could use a bit of freshening up, but mostly I need to pee, so the groceries will have to wait.

BLAKE

I DECIDE TO HELP PUT AWAY WHAT LOOKS LIKE ABOUT A TON of fruit. I wonder if she loves it that much or she's planning to take a fruit plate to the party tomorrow. I go to pick up one of those flimsy plastic shopping bags, and it falls open, spilling a few oranges onto the floor. One of the little renegades rolls over and ends up under the bed, so I chase it and try to nab it before it gets too far under. I reach down, and instead of grabbing the orange, I latch onto a stiff… something. Curious, I drag it out and… huh… It's a gym bag, and I can't help but wonder what it's doing squashed under her bed. Anyway, I ignore it and reach way under the bed to get the orange.

Once I have the orange, I go to slide the gym bag back in

place, and as I shove it, the opening gapes wide. It's obvious that the zipper is stuck and didn't close properly. But what this bag reveals nearly stops my heart.

This thing is holding thousands and *thousands* of dollars. Big, thick wads of twenty-dollar bills—at least from what I can see without rooting around in the bag. Instead of replacing it, I pull it the rest of the way out and heft it—and realize it must weigh around thirty to forty pounds. I'll have to do the math later to roughly guess at the amount. It dawns on me that she must have dug into this stash before hitting the Piggly Wiggly. She was paying with mostly twenties. I found that a tiny bit odd, but not nearly as odd as I'm finding it now! The bathroom tap turns off, so I shove the bag back under the bed. I grab the orange I retrieved as well as the ones by the table, and I'm just putting the bag of fruit into the fridge when Sloane reappears.

She's refreshed her makeup and brushed her hair. It's now loose from her former ponytail and flows around her shoulders. She is so gorgeous it almost hurts my eyes to look at her. I plaster on what I hope isn't a fake-as-shit grin and say, "You look beautiful." I mean what I say because she does look stunning, but I doubt my smile is reaching my eyes. *Who is this woman?*

What could she possibly be doing with this enormous stash of money? I can't just outright accuse her of anything because I was snooping, even if it was accidentally—sort of. I have no evidence that the money is the result of something shady, though it certainly has that look about it. I mean, who on earth keeps that kind of cash under their bed after arriving in a strange new town with no apparent purpose in mind? She also might have made up that silly story about meeting Tanner Lassiter in Southampton when she was little. Something smells fishy to me, and I'm going to figure it out. That means I need to keep a close eye on the lovely Ms. Morgan. I just hope I can remain professional because my attraction to her is off the charts.

"Thank you," she tells me in a soft, low voice. "You look pretty great yourself, Blake."

Uh oh. I'm so screwed. Just hearing her use that tone and say my name does all kinds of things to me. Below the belt things. *Stop it.*

She approaches me, and I'm relieved to see her going for a bag of frozen items that she stashes in her freezer. I was afraid she might be coming in for a kiss. I can't do that, can I? God, I sure as hell want to. She's a possible suspect though… of what, I have no idea.

Oh, heaven help me.

CHAPTER
Six

Sloane

Ever since I came out of the bathroom, something seems vaguely off with Blake, and I can't for the life of me figure out what could have happened in the few minutes I left him alone. Did he get a call from work? Is he just going cold again?

We decide to walk from my place to the tavern because it's so close—just a couple of blocks away. It's cooling off, so I grab a jacket from my closet, and he politely helps me into it, but it's as if he's suddenly afraid to touch me. I wonder what makes this man tick. He watches me closely as I use my key to lock the deadbolt as we head out. I'm sure he's concerned with security, given what he does.

The Hive is aptly named. It's a busy place for this time of

day, and conversation is buzzing around us—even though it's early and the live music isn't scheduled for a few more hours. Instead of regular bar shelves, the liquor bottles are stored in a huge honeycomb unit that makes me smile. A nice-looking man greets us from behind the bar as we walk in, and Blake introduces me to him. His name is Buford Wallace, the owner.

"I need another bartender," he grumbles. "My last one lit out of town with the woman who worked for Juni at Hot Stuff. They said they needed some adventure before settling down, whatever that meant. This isn't my job usually," he explains to me. "Know anyone who can mix cocktails?"

"Sorry, I don't. I just like drinking them."

He laughs a little and gets back to work pouring drinks. I wonder what it's like when this place is full. At least Buford has the help of another guy at the other end of the long bar.

Blake leads me to a table, and right away a cute waitress bounces up to ask what we'd like to drink and if we need anything to snack on. They don't serve dinner. We settle on beer and nachos because Blake suddenly professes that he's hungry, although I don't know how. Maybe I'll have one or two chips.

Boy, was I wrong. These nachos are the bomb. The beer is ice cold and goes down easy, and the nachos are just the right balance of flavor and heat, piled with yummy, gooey cheese and sides of the best guacamole and salsa I've ever had. Who knew Honeybee Hollow's Hive would turn out to be the nacho capital of the world? If I'm not careful, I won't be fitting into my skimpy shorts, and I'll have to go up a size in Hot Stuff t-shirts.

Blake seems to have loosened up, but he keeps asking me questions about home that I don't really feel like answering. I give bland answers and fire questions right back at him to deflect. He's friendly, but I also get the sense from him that he's not opening up with a lot of personal information.

So far, he knows I went to NYU and majored in theater arts. I told him I haven't made a big deal out of looking for parts to audition for because I didn't get a lot of encouragement from anyone, and I finally decided that maybe I was foolish and ought to have majored in something more practical, like business. But I'd love to start a small local theater company someday. In the back of my mind, I wonder if Honeybee Hollow would support something like that.

I discover that Blake joined the Marines right out of high school, and that paid his college tuition to study police science like he'd always wanted to do. He seems content to be sheriff now and looks forward to running the office the way he thinks it ought to be run. His deputies are somewhat unambitious guys, but they're good men. He's not surprised they were happy he was made sheriff instead of one of them—even if it was sort of a given since he was made chief deputy a couple of years ago. I get the sense these guys aren't the most dedicated lawmen you could find.

It's interesting that we both seem totally reticent to speak of family. I change the subject each time he brings up my home life, and I get the distinct impression that the subject of his family is a no-go zone. The only hint I get is when he tells me, "I'm not in touch with my parents," and he leaves it at that, changing the subject again. I'm intrigued to know more, but in learning more from him, I might be compelled to give away my story, and I'm not ready to do that either. If I don't pump him for information, perhaps he won't do that to me.

We're on our second beer when he gets a call he says he has to take as he sees the number on his phone. "I see. I'm so sorry," he says to the caller. "Thanks for letting me know… Yeah, alright." He disconnects and looks at me sadly. "They took Sheriff Hansen off life support, and he passed a little while ago."

"I'm sorry, Blake. Do you need to do anything?"

"I need to head over to the hospital. I'm sorry to cut this short, but his wife needs a ride home, and I can give her his box of stuff."

"Okay. I'll get home on my own. You need to go."

"Are you sure? I feel bad about this."

"It's fine, Blake. You need to go help a friend, and Honeybee Hollow seems like a safe enough place for me to walk two blocks by myself. I hear they have excellent law enforcement and low crime." I try for a smile.

"If you're sure. But be careful in any case. I'm really sorry to rush off."

"Do what you need to do, and I'll see you tomorrow," I tell him. I guess I could walk back to my apartment with him since his car is in front of Hot Stuff, but I'm just not inclined to at the moment. Let him think I'm sticking around and maybe socializing with more of the locals.

"Right. Goodnight, Sloane." He makes no mention of taking me to the party, so once again I'm feeling somewhat rejected—even if I was the one who turned down his last bland attempt to give me a ride. I thought we were flirting a bit—at least before we left my place, but maybe he was just being polite. Again with the whiplash. Then I remember him saying the sheriff's wife was surrounded by her friends at the hospital, and I wonder why one of them couldn't have driven her home. Oh well… it's not my place to ask that kind of question; it's not like he owes me an explanation.

Blake stands up, closes out the bill at the bar, and pushes out the door without a backward glance. I'm exhausted from a long day. Working at Hot Stuff means exceptionally early mornings, so I finish my beer and then head for home. Frankly, I'm mentally exhausted too. Riding a seesaw will do that to a person, I guess.

On my walk home, I decide that our conversation felt more like Blake was interrogating me than trying to get to know me better. I wonder if being a lawman makes a guy lose regular social skills. Eh… I shouldn't let him get to me.

IN THE MORNING, I HAVE TO FACE LOTS OF NOSY QUESTIONS about last night's "date" with Blake. It's incredible how quickly news spreads in this town. I downplay any romantic vibes and try unsuccessfully to let people know I just met the man, and we're only friends. The talk is also about the unfortunate loss of Sheriff Hansen—a man I never had the chance to meet. So I have little to say on that score other than I'm sorry it happened.

One particularly noisy trio of women arrive at Hot Stuff all smiling and winking at me. The loudest of them announces, "You're just the right woman for that poor, lonely boy. I can tell, Sloane!" Why she thinks she knows anything about me or why I'm perfect for anyone is beyond me, but it gets even weirder than that.

One of her buddies says, "A June wedding would be so lovely, don't you think? It's beautiful here then. You could get married in the park where we have the most perfect gazebo. It's gorgeous all covered in flowers and twinkle lights." But then she adds, "I run the flower shop around the corner. It's called Honey Bea's Blossoms; I'm Bea. When I came to this town a few years ago, I felt like it was fate that brought me here." She hands me a business card and gives me a wink. Now I understand her enthusiasm better, but it still makes me terribly uncomfortable.

Her friend laughs and chides her, "Don't get ahead of yourself, Bea. You're making Sloane blush. And besides… you have the *only* flower shop in town."

"Yes, lucky me. But we need more weddings," she pouts and then giggles.

I want to tell her not to hold her breath, but that seems rude. So I just smile, stuff the card in my pocket, and move onto other business. I'll toss out the card later—certainly not in front of her. I can't imagine being married to Sheriff Hot and Cold, but I don't tell her that either.

Later, Juni's in a hurry to get home and prepare for her party, so I assure her I can close up. We're closed tomorrow, so there isn't anything extra that needs to be done beyond the regular cleaning and locking up. We're finally alone in the shop for a moment when I ask, "Before you go, may I please have your address so I can look up directions to your house?"

"Sure, but what happened to Blake? Did we scare him off? Did something happen when you went to The Hive? Is he a bad kisser?"

So she's also heard the gossip and knows he and I were together last evening. "Frankly, Juni, I don't understand that man at all, and I certainly didn't kiss him. One minute he's all friendly and a little flirty, and the next minute he's all business and makes me feel like a suspect who's being interrogated… for what, I have no clue." She narrows her eyes at me in a contemplative manner, and I add, "When we were at the bar, he got a call and had to run. He left me alone in the bar without a backward glance. I know he felt that he had to go, but boy did that ever feel cold."

"What did you do?"

"A few minutes after he left, I got up and went home. I wasn't too interested in sitting there all by myself."

"Too bad. You might have met someone else. It would have served him right."

"Juni, I'm not looking, alright? It was just kinda nice when he was paying some attention to me. He's a man of mixed signals, though, that's for sure."

"Well, there will be plenty of guys at our place tonight. Levi's band, Wildflower Whiskey, has offered to play a while. Levi's married, as you know, but you should see the other guys in that band." She fans herself. "If I didn't have enough men in my life already, I'd get to know their drummer. They call him Banger, and I've always wondered how he got that nickname. It makes me think of banging on drums and also bangers… *sausages*… if you know what I mean." She winks. "Or he could be someone who likes to fuck indiscriminately too, I guess. He sure does love to take off his shirt, and he routinely tosses it out into the audience when he gets too hot. Anyhoo, he looks like fun."

I can't help laughing as her face turns red, and she continues to fan herself. "I'll keep that in mind." I plug her address into my phone so I can find the party. "Oh, do you mind if I borrow a platter from the kitchen? I'm bringing a fruit tray. I hope that's alright."

"Sure! You don't need to, but it's a great idea. Thanks. I'll see you later." And Juni is on her way out.

Fifteen minutes later, I turn the sign around and lock the

front door. I carefully clean up the tables, floor, and random messes around the kitchen, then lock the back door before heading upstairs where I am soon elbow-deep in chopping up fruit. Then it's a shower and picking out a fun outfit, and once again I'm heading to my car, this time laden with a fragrant platter of fresh fruit.

I'm honest enough with myself to admit that I'm disappointed Blake never called. I half expected him to show up before the party… but he doesn't.

CHAPTER
Seven

I FEEL LIKE A HEEL. A HYPOCRITE. A JERK. I'M SO ATTRACTED to Sloane I can't stand it, and I think I've been treating her terribly. No, there's no *thinking* about it; I *have* been treating her terribly. When I talk to her, it's obvious she's hiding something, but it's just as obvious to me that she doesn't have a devious mind or the heart of a criminal. But that sack of money is so weird! It has to be connected to something wrong —even if it's hard to believe she's a crook. No one who's honest keeps cash under their bed like that unless they're insane, and I don't get that vibe from her either.

So today I spent hours looking for her online and for anything associated with her name that might signal suspicious activity. Know what I found? Absolutely nothing. But it was the wrong kind of nothing. It's not that she doesn't have a social media presence or a criminal record—she doesn't even seem to exist. There are no records of a Sloane Morgan anywhere near her possible age. She doesn't have a driver's license, a car registration, any traffic tickets or misdemeanors. She doesn't have a passport or a Social Security number, and she hasn't been married or divorced anywhere. I wonder if she was born outside of the US, but she mentioned her parents having friends in Southampton, so that would generally locate her in New York or an adjacent state. I could kick myself for not jotting down her license plate number, but I don't want to go prowling around Hot Stuff and have Juni or Sloane catch me at it. I ran out of time to continue my hunt before I delved into school records at NYU, but I'll do that as soon as I can. Now I'm running late for Juni, Jack, and Asher's party, and I need to get ready. Oh crap! I hope Sloane wasn't expecting me to pick her up. I fucked that up too because I totally forgot about Juni volunteering me.

I feel like a complete scatterbrain between the new job and trying to figure out Sloane's story. If she seems miffed at me for forgetting her, I can always use the lame excuse that she turned me down when I offered her a ride. What a gentleman.

Before heading out to their place, I swing by Hot Stuff and don't see Sloane's car anywhere, so I guess she got to the party on her own after all. See? I'm a complete jackass. I hope she didn't wait around for me. I hope she isn't royally pissed at me for leaving her at The Hive last night. I didn't think anyone was going to hit on her after I left because they'd seen me with her.

Although… come to think of it, maybe me ditching her would have been a green light to anyone who saw her by herself. Either way, it was a dick move. I guess I'll have to own that and apologize.

By the time I get to their house, the place is packed, and cars are parked everywhere—which means I'd look like a weirdo hunting around for Sloane's so I can jot down her license plate. Deciding this isn't the time for sleuthing, I grab the booze I brought and head for the door.

Half the town is here already. I had no idea the three of them were so popular, but it makes sense, I guess. I'm sure all of them meet plenty of people in their jobs. The house is immense and gorgeous, and Levi and his band are playing at one end of a gigantic great room as I enter. I look around for Juni or her guys, but instead I see Sloane with her head too close to some asshole I don't know. She's laughing, and I guess it's good she's having fun, but it burns me up inside when he takes her hand and leads her to the middle of the room where quite a few couples are dancing the two-step. He carefully shows her the sequence of steps. She falters a couple of times, but then she takes off with him like she's been two-stepping for years. I can't help but admire how graceful she is. She's wearing a short, twirly sort of skirt that shows off those amazing legs of hers, and I'm dying to run my hand up…

"Better cut in, big fella, and stop shooting daggers with your eyes," a voice says in my ear. I turn and see Juni smirking at me.

"Uh, here. This is for you," I say, thrusting a bottle of fine Kentucky bourbon into her hands. "Thanks for inviting me."

"Thank you. Cheer up, Blake. She's just dancing with the guy, not marrying him."

"Humph," I grumble.

"Why didn't you bring her with you if you're so invested in her?"

"I'm not, uh… well, I screwed up, and… fuck, I have no idea." I don't know what to say, but apparently, I'm on Juni's radar about this. "Do you think she's mad at me now?"

"Depends on what you tell her and how well you grovel, big guy. I think she was hoping to be your date for the evening, but we didn't really get into it."

"So who's the guy with her? He doesn't look familiar."

"No idea. Sorry. He's probably someone Jack or Asher knows from work. He's sure good-looking though, and he's a great dancer. Do you two-step?" Juni gets sparkles in her eyes when she sees me grinding my teeth. She's definitely laughing at me. *Women!*

"Yes, Juni. I have been known to dance on occasion."

"Then get your ass out there before she goes and falls for that guy. Sheesh, Blake." She stares at me a second, sets down the bourbon on the nearest table, and grabs my hand. Before I know it, she's dragging me to the edge of their makeshift dance floor. They've rolled up the rug so we'd have hardwood to dance on, and the furniture is all pushed to the perimeter of the room. "Dance, you big goofball," she hisses at me. I take her loosely into my arms, and I don't know how she does it, but by sheer force of will she leads us closer and closer to Sloane and her partner. The song is coming to an end by the time we get there.

As the last notes dwindle away, we're right next to them, and Juni says loudly, "Hi, Sloane. You look so pretty tonight. Who's your handsome partner?" She bats her eyelashes and puffs up her impressive rack at the guy. Seriously?

Sloane looks baffled like she has no idea what his name is, but the guy eyes Juni with a lascivious look and sticks out his hand. "I'm Freddy." Juni takes his hand and whisks him away as another song starts up.

Unfortunately for Freddy, they only make it a few steps around the dancefloor when Asher cuts in saying, "Hey, Fred. I see you've met *my* woman." He bends down from his towering height and lays a scorching kiss on her. Ol' Freddy slinks away, and I see that Sloane is stifling a laugh. God, she's breathtaking.

"Uh, wanna dance?" I ask her while she's still smiling and before Freddy can make his way back to her to try to reclaim what he so swiftly gave up for another pretty face. She cocks her head at me in consideration, so I say, "Please?" Lucky for me, it's another two-step I'm pretty sure I can handle okay, so when she doesn't say no, I take her hand, wrap my other around her, and off we go. Dancing with Sloane seems effortless because we're instantly in sync with one another.

As the song winds down, I see Juni hurry over to Levi and whisper something to him. Before the current song is a memory, the band heads immediately into a slow number, and I smile, wrapping Sloane in closer to me. She doesn't seem to have any objection. And, wow, does she feel good.

The song must be one of Wildflower Whiskey's new originals because it doesn't sound familiar, but it sure is great. It's all about misunderstood new love and hopefulness. Levi's incredible voice overflows with emotion as he belts it out, and as I look around the room, I see that conversation has stopped so everyone can listen to him. Sometimes I wish I had a talent like he has for singing, or his partner Sklyer's talent with a brush and a canvas. It seems instead that my superpower is fucking up with women. I firm up my hold on Sloane and bring her into me a little closer. I'm gratified when she lays her head against me. Holding her goes from feeling good to feeling right and perfect.

What am I doing? I'm so attracted to her I'm losing all sense of propriety. She might be a fugitive, a drug dealer, or a scam artist, or maybe she's fleeing for her life.

I need to find out. Soon.

CHAPTER
Eight

WHAT AM I *DOING* ALL SNUGGLED UP TO GORGEOUS SHERIFF Change-His-Mind? He smells delicious, and his strong arms feel so good around me, I want to stay cocooned like this forever. My stupid head plunked itself onto his warm, hard chest like it had a magnetic pull. And Blake seems just as comfortable laying his cheek against my hair. Hmm… interesting. I'm so comfy like this, I'm not even irritated at Juni for manipulating the situation. I was ready for a reprieve from that other guy. Nice to look at, but a giant airhead. And I didn't miss her asking Levi to sing this song. It's sure a long one, but so moving and beautiful. I don't want it to end. Since when do I act like this?

I pull back a little and look up into Blake's eyes. They're burning into mine with blazing heat. I swear he'd like to close the distance and kiss me, but I'm not ready for that in front of half the town. The residents would start naming our kids before the night is over. To lighten the mood a bit, I ask, "What do you call people from Honeybee Hollow? Honeybees? Hollowers, Honeymooners?"

Blake smiles and says, "I wondered that too when I first arrived. The other deputies tried to convince me they called themselves Hivers, but that didn't sound right to me, especially after I tried using the term a few times and got nothing but blank stares. So I asked around to some other folks who seemed in the know and came up with zilch. I guess they just refer to themselves as townsfolk or neighbors. Maybe we ought to start a trend." He winks at me, and I go gooey inside until he announces, "I vote for Hollow Heads or, no—just Mooners." I snort in the most unladylike manner and then start laughing. He's grinning at me like I invented humor as he continues, "We could spread Mooners around and never take credit for it—you know… saying we heard it somewhere from someone. Then in a couple of generations it will be like the word Hoosier for residents of Indiana with no plausible explanation whatsoever. That will make people speculate and come up with crazy theories that become part of its history. What do you think?"

I finally stop laughing when it dawns on me that the music stopped a while ago, and we're still in each other's arms in the middle of an empty dance floor. Levi and the other band members are gone. How long have we been standing here like this anyway?

I try to step back a little, but Blake's arms are firm, so I ask, "Would you like to get something to eat or drink? I think the dancing is over for now."

Blake swivels his head around, apparently just as clueless as I am, and whispers, "Oops," with a soft laugh. We go and fill plates from the buffet table with all kinds of yummy-looking items and grab a couple of beers. It's a lovely clear night, but still a bit chilly, so I'm relieved when we find a vacant loveseat outside in a covered area next to a space heater. The landscaping out here is amazing and artistically lit, and several folks are chatting away clustered around a large firepit. This house was definitely built for entertaining.

"I'm curious to know more about you, Sloane," Blake says as we get comfortable. He has an affectionate look of interest on his face this time, so I feel less as if I'm being interrogated.

I try to relax, take a deep breath, and answer, "Well... I was born in New York but went to boarding school in New Jersey, so I was really only home on holidays and in the summer. My parents thought sending me away to school would civilize me or something. I already told you about college. I'm not all that interesting, I guess. I like theater and movies."

"Don't sell yourself short, Sloane. I think you're plenty fascinating. Do you think you'd really like to start a community theater company here in town? I've thought about how you mentioned that. I bet folks would love it; we have nothing like that now, you know. You could have classes for kids, put on variety shows or plays, and have the locals act. It would be great! I bet people in all of the other towns around here would support something like that too, once the word got out."

"Wow. Um, thanks for your vote of confidence. It would be a lot of fun if there was a place I could use."

"Don't local theater companies often use school auditoriums?"

"Oh, um, I guess so. Do you know anyone on the school board I could talk to?"

He chuckles at me and answers, "Sloane, I'm the sheriff. I know everyone. If you're serious, let me make a few calls for you and find out who's in charge."

"You'd do that for me?"

"Of course. And you should know, this town loves to volunteer for local events. You could get all kinds of groups to help you with stage sets, costumes, whatever. I bet this community would open their arms and embrace this idea with enthusiasm. Everyone wants to be entertained and to be a part of something fun, and they all love to jump in and participate. Maybe ticket sales could raise money for charity, and people would love that even more."

We continue on in this vein, and it turns out Blake has some very helpful ideas. A tiny spark burns and grows inside of me. Could my crazy idea be possible in this sweet little burg? I never could have made much headway in New York where there was way too much competition, and I didn't have the credentials to back me up. But here? It's a whole new world. I could do this!

We talk and talk, and I lose all track of time until Jack makes his way toward us and sits down on the chair next to the loveseat.

"How are the two of you doing? Having fun?" he asks with a big grin. I can see why Juni is with both Jack and Asher. They're great guys and definitely easy on the eye.

"Yeah, thanks for having us," Blake answers enthusiastically.

"It's a great party, Jack. Is Levi's band going to play anymore?" I ask hopefully, thinking about being in Blake's arms. "I'd love to dance some more." I suddenly realize their "break" has been terribly long. And I don't remember hearing them say they'd play more later—even if I was so wrapped up in what Blake was saying that I didn't even notice they'd quit.

Jack grins and shakes his head. "Sorry. They all went home about an hour ago. Levi and Skyler thought Brooke was looking tired and needed some rest." He gets a soft look on his face and adds, "It's beautiful the way those two guys watch out for her. Well… and for each other."

"Oh, I'm sorry we didn't get to visit with them more. Is Brooke doing alright?"

"She swore she was fine and teased her guys about actually wanting to go home because they were horny. But I agree, she looked pretty exhausted. I can't imagine what being pregnant would feel like. Phew." Jack shakes his head, and his blond hair flops over his forehead in a way that makes him look younger than I'm sure he has to be. What a cutie.

I look around and realize we're among the last stragglers who haven't left yet and suddenly say, "Jack, can we do anything to help clean up? I didn't know it was so late."

"Thanks for offering, Sloane, but we have a staff of people who'll take care of it. You just enjoy." He smiles and stands up.

Taking a cue from him—and the silence around us that tells me it's not just the band that has gone home—I also stand and say, "It's time for us to go, Blake. These wonderful hosts of ours are probably exhausted. Thank you so much for the terrific party, Jack. Is Juni around so I can say good night?"

"Last I saw of her, she and Asher were making out in the kitchen." He looks past us and adds, "Oh, never mind. Here she comes after all."

I turn to see Juni strolling up to us with a knowing grin on her face. She asks, "Did you kids finally kiss and make up?"

My face turns hot, and I steal a glance at Blake who narrows his eyes at her for a second before saying, "Thanks for having us, Juni. It's been a great party, and now I think I'll make sure Sloane makes it home safely."

We all hug and say our goodnights and our thanks about five more times because no one can ever break away without that rigmarole. Eventually, I'm heading out toward my car with Blake, who has taken my hand. It feels so nice. When was the last time anyone wanted to hold my hand? Such a simple thing, and so comforting.

We're standing in the moonlight by the driver's side of my car when I decide I'm curious, so I ask Blake, "This place is amazing, and this party was so decadent; I thought Jack ran an art gallery, and the others don't seem like they're making millions in cryptocurrency. If I'm not being too nosy, how do they afford all of this?"

Blake smiles and answers, "It's not a secret that Jack's the sole heir to an enormous family fortune because of the family's corporation, but he's also already received a rather huge inheritance from his grandparents. He's pretty open about it because some jerk of a reporter did a big magazine article about his gallery and spilled the beans about his family. He was thrilled that the article did so much for his gallery but pretty pissed about the rest. Anyway, he doesn't try to be secretive; it would be pointless. To everyone around here, he's just Jack Hartz, partner of Juniper Barry *and* Asher Bellamy. They're terrific people and well-loved by the community. He does a lot for local artists and gives back to the town in many ways." Blake slips his arm around me and adds, "I understand Juni and Asher were unaware of Jack's wealth until they'd already been involved for several months. So they already loved him. I think that's admirable and shows their character."

"Wow. I didn't realize, and Juni certainly never mentioned Jack's status. They all seem so nice; I'm happy for them."

Blake chuckles and asks, "Do you think you could ever be in that kind of a relationship?"

"With two guys at once?" He nods at me, and I state emphatically, "No. I have a hard enough time managing one man at a time. It wouldn't be my thing. What about you?"

"Not ever. I've been a jealous jerk in relationships, and I'd never be able to share with another guy, have sex when another guy was near me, *or* be interested in two women at once. So threesomes aren't on my radar. I guess it works great for the right folks though."

"You get jealous?"

"Sloane, I'm not even in a relationship with you, and I wanted to stomp that weasel you were dancing with into the ground."

My jaw drops, and I gape at him before asking, "Why?"

He takes a deep breath and pauses a moment, skewering me with his eyes. Before I can react, he's kissing me. Umm… I'm shocked for about two seconds, but the feel of his mouth on mine is amazing. This is so far from a "getting to know you" kind of kiss, it's ridiculous. This is the kind of kiss you experience when someone's about to fuck you senseless. He's rough and possessive, and I feel like he's somehow conquering me—even though I wasn't putting up any resistance. I've never been kissed with such enthusiastic and overwhelming desire in my life. There was no shyness or easing into this—just an attack of lust and command. His arms tighten around me as I open my mouth to accept him in. My

God, I've never…! My breathing accelerates, and I wrap my arms around him, clutching at his shirt as if to bring him closer, but he's already as close as he can be. His hardness digs into me, and suddenly I lose it in a fit of laughter.

"Sheriff, are you packing a loaded gun in your pocket?" I can't help asking. I know it's corny, but the mental image is more than I can take.

"Very funny, my beautiful Sloane. It's pretty obvious what you do to me. Now stop laughing so I can enjoy this some more."

"Yes, si—" I start to say, but his mouth is on me again. His chest is hard against my sensitive breasts as I rub on him like a wanton cat. I tingle everywhere. Heat and desire build up in my body so quickly, I suddenly wonder if I could have an orgasm just from kissing. Our tongues battle, but I'm losing ground and don't care. I love being captured and possessed by him. I'm breathless by the time he pulls back.

I can't read the expression on his face. Yes, it's mostly dark out, but the moon illuminates us. He looks thoughtful and maybe a little angry—at what, I can't imagine. His normally bright blue eyes are so dilated, they're nearly black. But then he gives me a completely different kind of kiss. The kind you give someone you've known for years, and you're leaving for work. Closed mouth, no tongue. Friendly, but nearly clinical.

"Get some sleep, Sloane," he tells me. "Good night." And he turns away and strides to his car without a backward glance.

I stand there for a moment, blinking, frozen in place. "Well, that was weird," I mutter to myself as I climb into my car. I put my fingers to my lips, still buzzing from his heavy-handed attention. I shake my head a little and head for home. Blake has already hit the road just ahead of me, so I follow his taillights until he turns down a narrow road away from the downtown area.

He is so unpredictable, I don't know what to think now.

CHAPTER
Nine

BLAKE

WHAT WAS I THINKING? I ZEROED IN ON THOSE GORGEOUS, kissable lips of hers and acted like I was going to devour them. Devour *her*. I couldn't stop myself, even though I told myself all night not to get carried away. That woman is hiding some-thing or I'm a monkey's uncle. But I can't help acting like a love-struck teenager with raging hormones if she's in the same room as me. And I was dumb enough to even admit it to her. Oh shit. My brains were so scrambled after kissing the daylights out of her, I forgot to look at her license plate *again*. I'm a terrible sheriff if I can get so distracted by a beautiful woman.

But it's not just that she's so pretty. There are lots of good-looking women in Honeybee Hollow. This one makes me want to tattoo my name on her forehead so everyone will know she belongs to me! What the fuck? I've never acted like this—even with my former fiancée. We broke up, and I felt a huge sense of relief, even though I thought I'd loved her. Now I can't stop thinking about a woman I'm barely acquainted with who has all kind of mystery about her. She could be a terrible person for all I know. What's wrong with me?

One thing is for sure. I need to get to the bottom of what's up with Sloane Morgan as soon as possible.

I head for the shower to take care of the persistent stiffness that made driving home awkward—hating myself because *all* I can think of is Sloane. I stroke my junk and moan her name like she's right next to me as I coat the shower wall with my release. Shaking my head, I clean up the mess only to get hard again as the memory of her mouth against mine fills my head. Those incredible tits of hers were plastered to my chest and felt just right. Oh, for crying out loud. I need to stroke myself again to get rid of the image, and I grunt as I explode one more time. *Cut it out. You're objectifying her, and she isn't someone you need to get involved with. You need to stay away and figure out where all of that damn money came from. But, oh, those gorgeous long legs of hers. What I wouldn't do to have them wrapped around me as I slam into… stop it*! I turn on the cold tap and finally begin to come back to earth.

Now if I can just keep her out of my head long enough to fall asleep, I'll be a happy man.

That plan doesn't work.

THE NEXT DAY IS SUNDAY, AND I WAKE UP LATE AND BLEARY-eyed. I'm not expected at the office today, thank heaven. I hardly slept at all, fantasizing about Sloane and what I'd love to do with her. I have it bad, and this pisses me off. I am not looking to get involved, especially with someone of dubious character.

But what do I do? I drink about a gallon of coffee with my hearty breakfast and start thinking of people I can talk to who could help Sloane with her local theater idea. Do I try to figure out more about who the hell she is? No. That would be the wise move, but so far, I'm not so smart when it comes to her. By noon, I've locked down three different people in the community who think her plan has terrific merit and tell me to have her contact them. Their enthusiasm is infectious, and I finally feel buoyant about having her in town instead of worried about it.

Then it occurs to me that I don't have a phone number for her. Juni must have Sloane's number, but I don't want to bother her after last night's party. She and her men are probably exhausted. So I do the most sensible thing. I wolf down a fast sandwich, take another shower, put on a clean shirt and jeans, and head over to Sloane's apartment.

This time, I act like I'm checking my phone and take a quick photo of her car's plate. I'm a bit surprised the plate is from Kentucky. I pocket my phone and head up the stairs to her place.

I knock on the door, and right away Sloane answers, surprised to see me. She doesn't open the door very wide, and my instant thought is that she might be hiding some guy inside from my view. However, just in case I'm jumping to conclusions, I plaster on what I hope is a friendly smile and say, "Hi Sloane. I have some information for you that will help your project we talked about—in case you actually want to pursue it. But I realized I don't have your phone number, so I thought I'd come over and deliver it myself. May I come in?" Could I babble anymore? Sound like a bigger dweeb? Why isn't she opening the door? Is someone in there?

"Oh, um… okay. Thanks, Sheriff." She slowly steps back and opens the door wider.

Sheriff? Not this again. Is she pissed at me, or does she have a guilty conscience about something? I can't help scanning the room for someone else, but not only is she alone, there is an amazing aroma of something cooking permeating the air. "Wow. It smells great in here, Sloane."

She smiles sweetly and says, "I've been making soup. It's done now, and I was about to have some for lunch. Care to join me? I can never make a small amount."

I never turn down food, so I say, "Oh, well, that's really nice of you considering I just showed up unannounced, but I'd love some." I shuck off my jacket, pull a piece of notepaper out of my pocket with names and numbers on it, and settle myself at her small table. She places a large, steamy bowl of soup in front of me with a crusty roll beside it. "This looks wonderful. Do you cook a lot?"

"I do, actually, when I have the chance, and it's so dreary and chilly today, soup sounded like the perfect thing to make." She sits down across from me, and I slide the list over to her.

"Here you go. And before I leave, would you mind giving me your number?"

"Thank you. It looks like you've done your homework. But, um… why?"

"Why? Because I like you. I thought that was pretty obvious last night. I wanted to help you out, and I'd like to be able to get in touch with you. That is, unless you have something against me. But you seemed pretty friendly last night." What kind of game is this woman playing? Although I'll admit I did leave her in a rush when I was afraid I was going to take things too far. Not cool.

"Honestly, Blake, you confuse me. One second you're all over me, and the next it's like I have cooties." Her beautiful brown eyes look so serious, and I feel like a jerk. I have to look away. "Last night was another example of you running off like you feel guilty about being around me or something. I like you too, but this is just weird behavior."

"I'm so sorry. Truth is, I was afraid I was getting a little too turned on." I admire her blush and clear my throat to change the subject. "Do you think we could get to know each other better? I enjoy talking to you, but I get this impression all the time that you're holding something back. It has me a little worried, to tell you the truth." This feeling is heightened when her face goes even pinker, and she looks away.

She levels a look at me and says, "I could say the same, Blake. Other than you're the new sheriff, I know next to nothing about you or your background. Juni mentioned that you were a Marine, but that's it. Where did you grow up? What's your family like? Why did you want to be in law enforcement? I'd probably be more open about my life if it was a two-way street. I get the feeling from you sometimes I'm being interrogated, and I have no idea why. Are you just practicing on me in case some actual criminal shows up in town?"

Is this chick that good of an actor? She did study theater arts. Or maybe there's a perfectly good reason to have a stash of money hidden under her bed. Hah! As if. I'll call her bluff and tell her things about me I never, ever talk about. Maybe she'll open up to me then. It might be worth a shot.

"Okay, Sloane. Here's the unvarnished truth about my life. It's not a particularly pretty story, and no one else around here knows, so I'd appreciate it if you didn't feed it to the gossips. I'm not ashamed, or looking for pity, but it's *my* story—not anyone else's to pick apart and make judgments about." I have a couple of mouthfuls of soup and let that sink in for a moment. "The soup is delicious, by the way." It's full of fresh veggies and chunks of meat, but the herbs or spices or whatever she added for flavor are incredible.

"I was born not too far from here on the outskirts of a little hick town. I was the son of a teenage mother and some unknown asshole who drifted through the area where she lived with her mother. I don't remember her or any of my time before I was placed in foster care. My mother and grandmother died in a house fire, according to my case file, but the firemen found me wandering around outside. I must have been about two and a half. I went on to live with at least eight different foster families throughout the county—some longer and some only for a couple of days before they decided I was too much trouble, or I ate too much. I was always hungry, and the complaints were always the same when I was returned to the social worker. 'He eats too much.'

"When I was fourteen, I got picked up by a cop when I shoplifted a bag of cookies and some jerky from a gas station. The cop probably took one look at my pants that were too short, the holes in my sneakers, and the fact that I didn't have a jacket even though it was January, and he put me in his cruiser and drove me to a diner. He bought me a roast beef dinner with all the trimmings and had a long chat with me while I shoveled food into my mouth. It was the best meal I'd ever tasted.

"Basically, he said I could fulfill the lowest expectations placed on a foster kid and wind up in juvenile detention and then ultimately prison, or I could wise up, stop stealing, and get a job if I needed spending money. He told me how he studied hard in school instead of slacking off, then joined the Marines, and ultimately got his college degree. He made the Marines sound pretty exciting, and he seemed like a real badass. I wanted to be just like him. When I was done eating, he piled me back into the cruiser and took me to a thrift store where he found a parka and some gloves for me before taking me home. When we got there, he also had a chat with my foster mother about neglect and losing her rights to foster anyone. He told her he'd be keeping an eye on me and letting social services know that he had concerns. She needed to buy me some decent shoes and clothes with the support money she received.

"Before he left, he suggested places I could get after-school jobs, and he said he'd check on me every couple of weeks. Sometimes he'd take me on patrol, and when he had free time, we'd shoot hoops at the community rec center. He kept his promise to look in on me regularly until he…" I pause for a moment, making sure I can keep my voice controlled. "Well… when I was seventeen, he was run over by a drunk driver while he was giving a traffic ticket. Losing him was the worst thing that ever happened to me. He was the first person who ever gave a damn whether I lived another day, and my only real friend. So I vowed I'd make him proud and avenge wrongdoings by studying police science—if I lived through the Marine Corps." I shovel in some more soup. Sloane is looking at me with interest, but I'm glad it's not pity I see in her eyes.

"He sounds like a wonderful man. What was his name?"

"Officer Grover James. He let me call him Grover. He was only thirty-three years old and engaged to be married." I feel the sting of tears behind my eyes as I see his smiling face in my mind. He was a tall man like me, but that's where the physical similarity ended. He was as dark as I am fair. Close-cropped curls to my floppy dark-blond locks perpetually in need of a haircut. Expressive eyes so dark, they looked almost black to my icy blue ones. Grover was strong and proud, and he made me want to stand up straighter each time we inter-acted. When he laughed deep from his chest—with me, not ever at me—I felt like I'd won the lottery.

I snap out of this sad reverie as Sloane says, "I'm glad you seem to have lived through the Marines just fine, Blake. How did you end up in Honeybee Hollow? It's probably not a hotbed of criminal activity to fight."

I sure hope that's true. "I wanted a better job than what I was doing in Cumberland after graduating from college. Honeybee Hollow needed a deputy, and I fulfilled the require-ments. Simple as that. It's not glamorous, but this is a great little town, and I could have done a lot worse. Oh, and moving here helped make my engagement fall apart, so I haven't been involved with anyone in over three years. That's my life in a nutshell."

"You were engaged—what happened, if you don't mind me asking?"

"No, it's okay. At first, she didn't like me *telling* her we were moving to Honeybee Hollow, and that was probably not the best way I could have handled letting her know about my new job, but I quickly discovered the reason she was so dead set on staying in Cumberland. While I was out working, she was getting it on with a neighbor. When that came to light, I couldn't get out of there fast enough."

"Oh, I'm sorry, Blake."

"It was for the best. A big blow to the old ego though."

"It probably was for the best. Cheaters are gonna cheat, you know? It doesn't seem to matter to them how great the person is who's with them, they're always looking for something new and shiny just for grins." She looks me square in the eye and says, "She made a huge mistake, if you ask me. You seem like one of the good ones." Then she looks more speculative and adds, "I just can't figure out why you run so hot and cold all the time."

I wish I could explain it myself.

SLOANE

I think Blake is about to tell me more about his life before coming to Honeybee Hollow, but instead he asks, "So what's your story, Sloane? I know *how* you picked our lovely town to relocate to, but not what precipitated the move here in the first place. You've mentioned Southampton, and as nice as it is here, I doubt we hold a candle to that area. So, why are you here?"

Well, isn't that just the question? Why? How do I answer that without giving too much away? Or should I simply trust him and hope that if I need help down the road, he'll be there for me? Would it even be fair to drag him into my drama? I give him a thoughtful look while my brain churns with doubt and possibilities. But then I think how he has made his life a testament to someone who took a chance on him when he did something wrong simply because he was so hungry.

"Southampton was just where we went for the summer," I begin. "My parents had an apartment on the Upper East Side in New York for the rest of the time." He doesn't say anything, so I stand and clear away the dishes. "Would you like some coffee? This is a complicated story, so we might as well get comfortable."

"No thanks, I'm good." Blake stands and carries the rest of the dishes to the sink.

I grab a couple waters and make a plate of cookies that I set on the table in front of the couch. I sit and ask him to join me.

"I, um… this is so hard to talk about, Blake. I hope you won't judge me too harshly." Unfortunately, he has a grim expression on his face that I don't like a bit. He's judging me already, and I haven't even said anything yet. I notice his eyes flick over toward my bed a few times, and I can't help but wonder about that. Does he want to go to bed with me and hopes that can happen? He's delusional if he thinks this is the way to get me in the mood.

Finally, I bite the bullet and start to talk. I do need help, so I may as well try to make him a friend and confidant. And, with no small amount of surprise, I realize that I do trust him.

"My father owns what was a chain of extremely successful pizza restaurants and a delivery service. He started it with his brother years ago until his brother got tired of it and wanted to retire early to Florida. My dad bought him out and then apparently regretted it because running the business alone wasn't his strong suit, and the buyout left him strapped for cash. Unbeknownst to me, the business started losing money, and because he's a proud man, he didn't want to admit to his failure. I thought everything was going just fine, although in retrospect, my dad was visibly stressed out. I was living in my own apartment, so I guess I just didn't notice it much.

"One day, my dad called me and told me I needed to come to dinner at their place and wear something nice. He said he had someone coming he wanted me to meet, and I'd really enjoy myself if I came. So I agreed, I mean... why not, right? I had no reason to distrust him. When I got there, I noticed they had pulled out all the stops. Fine wine with dinner, a terrific meal, and my parents were all dressed up. They had a guest, of course, who turned out to be a guy a few years older than me—fairly handsome and uber polite. Just the kind of person my parents loved. His name was Sal Caputo. He immediately took notice of me in a big way, and my parents seemed both relieved and pleased.

"After that night, Sal started courting me and showering me with expensive gifts. And when I say expensive, I mean he gave me jewelry that was so outrageous, it was stuff I'd *never* want to put on. He sent me designer dresses to wear out to dinner and basically acted like he wanted to be my sugar daddy or something. I told him repeatedly I couldn't accept those things, but they kept coming. Aside from the ridiculous gifts, he seemed like a nice enough guy, and he was a fairly entertaining date, so I went out with him several times. Boy, was I an idiot. Even though I still felt as if I knew close to nothing of substance about the guy, after about two and a half months he *proposed*, telling me he'd cleared it with my dad already and that we had his blessing. When I said I'd have to think about it, he crammed this enormous and horribly gaudy diamond ring on my finger and said, 'Wear this while you're thinking, baby, but don't take too long.' It felt almost like a threat.

"The next day, my dad called and ordered me to marry Sal. He said it was important, and I needed to help the family and accept the proposal. I was shocked. I told him the proposal was too fast, and I wasn't in love with Sal. So then my mom got into it and started pressuring me as well. My parents wanted me to quit my job and focus on pleasing Sal. I asked them what was up and discovered that their business was failing because my dad wasn't good at running it without his brother, and they needed a new 'partner.' This was news to me. They were desperate, they told me; they'd already borrowed money from Sal, and all he wanted in return was to make me happy. It sounds crazy now, I know, but... they're my parents, and they were scared and upset. I didn't know how to just say no.

"I thought a compromise might be to move in with Sal to see how compatible we could be instead of actually marrying him, so I told him that. Sal's answer was no, but he bought me a Maserati for what he called a wedding gift, so I wouldn't have to get around on the subway." I notice Blake's eyebrows shoot up, so I laugh and say, "I know, right? A Maserati!" I shake my head and roll my eyes. "Sal said it was marriage or nothing, but he claimed he couldn't live without me, and he also wanted me to quit working so I could concentrate on what was important—him. The gifts were offensive to me at that point because he seemed to think the only way to my heart was by spending money on me.

"Soon, my mother started calling me with wedding plans. Apparently, Sal agreed to foot the bill and had most of the arrangements already made. It was like the three of them were a united front to take over my life, and I felt completely trapped. My dad came to see me, and I realized then how stressed he looked—like he'd aged a good fifteen years suddenly. He convinced me that Sal would make a great husband, and he needed Sal as a son-in-law in the worst way. He was so pitiful and convincing I almost agreed. He said Sal had a great head for making money, and he would get them out of all kinds of trouble; I just had to agree to marry him. My father stressed over and over that Sal would give me the moon because he was so crazy about me.

"The next night, I went out with Sal, and he acted like he was pouring his heart out to me over dinner and kept calling me 'baby,' but I still had my doubts about him. In retrospect, what he said was a lot of nothing. Still, wanting to protect my family from losing their livelihood, I agreed to marry Sal. Frankly, I was feeling boxed in a corner by the whole thing and hoped I could buy some time by agreeing then and later saying no. He seemed overjoyed and leaned in to kiss me, but I felt no spark at all. However, things got way worse than that.

"On the way back to my place, Sal said we needed to make a stop, and it was important that I come along. He was cheerful about it. So we pulled up to this house, and he escorted me up to the door. I thought I might be meeting someone in his family or something, so I wasn't all that concerned. He rang the bell, and as soon as we heard footsteps approaching the door, he pulled out a gun, thrust it into my hand, and raised it up, aiming at the door. When the door opened, he dropped his hand and left me shaking all over with this stupid gun in my hand. The guy who lived there immediately said, 'I have it right here, Sal. Don't let her shoot me!' He handed over a sack and slammed the door. Meanwhile, Sal laughed and hollered at him, 'Pleasure doin' business with you! See you next week.' He grabbed the gun back and steered me back to the car—not too gently, I might add, but he did tell me, 'You did great, baby.' I was terrified to say a word. I've never held a gun, much less pointed one at a person! Fortunately, he was quiet for the rest of the ride home, and I had time to calm down a little and form a plan.

"When we got back, Sal tried to get all romantic and wanted to spend the night with me. He was all jacked up and sweaty, and it made me kind of sick. This would have been our first time having sex, but I was so terrified of him because of the stunt he pulled with that gun, I summoned up every bit of acting training I'd learned in college and pretended to be terribly disappointed when I told him it was my time of the month, and I didn't want our first time spoiled by that. He readily agreed and said we'd revisit our consummation in a couple of days. But before he left, he said, 'We're as good as married now, baby, and will be in a few days, so don't get any crazy ideas about backing out now. Besides, the invitations have all gone out. One word of advice—when we fuck, I get extra turned on if you call me by my title, capo. It'll make everything that much sexier.' I had no idea what he meant, but then he said something even worse: 'I'll get you your own gun and teach you how to use it properly. You'll like it. Trust me, it's a real rush when you pull the trigger.' I tried everything to look calm throughout all of this debacle so he wouldn't suspect my real thoughts. I even told him having a gun sounded exciting, and I couldn't wait to be married to him. I might have poured it on a *little* heavy, but I played up to his ego so he wouldn't suspect my true feelings. I deserved a Tony award for that performance, believe me.

"The minute he left, I packed up everything I could fit into boxes and suitcases and loaded up the trunk of the Maserati. It was the wee hours of the morning by then, and I kept looking over my shoulder, worried someone might see me. But I didn't see a soul and didn't think anyone followed me as I started driving south. I didn't tell anyone where I was going—my parents, friends… no one. I did leave a message for my landlord that the rent money and the apartment key were on the kitchen table, and I would not be coming back. When I got to Pennsylvania, I found a hairdresser and a place that sells contact lenses, then I located a dealership in Philadelphia, sold the Maserati, and bought a crappy used Toyota. I had been worried the Maserati may have been tracked, so I couldn't get away from that monstrosity fast enough. Obviously, there was a *lot* left over after that transaction, and they were surprised but accommodating when I wanted it all handled in cash. Maybe the dealer was used to exceptionally rich people doing weird stuff; I don't know. At least they didn't accuse me of stealing the car or anything because the title was clearly in my name. After that, I stopped in several cities where I could get rid of the designer clothes and the ridiculous jewelry. I bought a new phone with a new number, copied a few favorite photos, ran over my original phone with my car for good measure, and heaved the wreckage into Chesapeake Bay in case it had some sort of tracking app I didn't know about. Eventually, I traded the Toyota for a much nicer Honda, and I paid cash for everything along the way. I'd always heard that credit cards could be traced, and even though no one I knew had access to my bank account or Visa, I wanted to be safe. I was… *am* so paranoid.

"Eventually, I made it to Honeybee Hollow, and as soon as I drove down Main Street, I finally felt like I could take a full breath of air.

"I won't be someone's chattel, Blake. If my father made terrible business decisions, that's on him. He treated me like I was invisible for most of my life until he needed me to seal a business deal. And Sal scares the crap out of me. He tosses money around like it's nothing, and I can't help but wonder what on earth he's really into. I suspect, though, that my father's pizza delivery business is a great opportunity for him to run some kind of illegal delivery service. I'm sorry if my mother is sucked into it, but she was also party to the conspiracy to get me married off to the rich guy. I won't have it. I wouldn't be surprised if he's killed people because I heard on the news later that there was a murder, and it sounded like it was possibly at the house where he took me when he threatened that man at gunpoint.

"So now I'm scared to death they'll find me and haul me back." I look at Blake, who is sitting beside me with a stoic expression, and ask, "What do you think?"

He takes a deep breath looks me in the eye and answers, "Well… I wondered where all the money came from. Now I know."

"You *what*? How did you know about the money? You were snooping?"

"It was an accident. I dropped an orange the other day

after bringing your groceries up here, and it rolled under your bed. When I went to fish it out, I rammed my hand into your gym bag. I dragged it out of the way to get to the orange because I didn't want to leave it—the orange—under your bed. When I went to shove the bag back in place, the top gaped open because the zipper was stuck, and I saw the stacks of cash. It shocked the daylights out of me because I figured you had something in there like your tennis gear or whatever. I'm really sorry, Sloane, but I wasn't trying to snoop, and maybe I can help you now that I know the story. I believe what you've told me to be true."

My stomach drops as I realize the implications of what he's saying. "But… wait a minute. You flirted and kissed the daylights out of me, and all that time you didn't trust me and thought I might be up to something shady because I was sleeping on a pile of cash? Was that just a way to get closer to me to figure out what was going on with me?"

Blake's face goes a little red, and he looks embarrassed. *Good.* "Sloane, I barely knew you, and I'm a trained officer of the law. It's my job to be skeptical of something that seems off. But on the other hand, there wasn't anything about the way you acted that gave me red flags about your character. I think in my heart of hearts, I knew there was a logical explanation, even though it looked as weird as fuck. You've told me your story, and I trust that it all happened the way you said. That said, however, you are in some possible danger, and I'm in a position to help you. And I really like you."

I glare at him for a moment until I realize he's absolutely right. The zipper did jam when I got the money out to go grocery shopping, and I didn't bother to fix it. Also, I do need help, and I'm scared to death. Without thinking, I crawl into his arms and snuggle against his big warm body. "Help me then," I whisper. "I'm afraid Sal is in the Mafia."

CHAPTER
Eleven

BLAKE

"I WOULDN'T BE TOO SURPRISED," I TELL HER. "ESPECIALLY since he called himself 'capo.'" Sloane seems pretty astute about this Caputo character. But I have to ask, "Is your name really Sloane Morgan?"

"Well, sort of. My given name is Anna Morgan Sloane. In college, everyone called me Sloane, and I liked it, so I decided to keep that. I've never felt like an Anna; it's too Victorian or something for me—even though that's what my family and all of my old friends call me. I know at some point all of this is likely to tumble down around me like a house of cards, but for now, I feel safe enough. I should also tell you that I'm normally a blue-eyed blonde—I got rid of the highlights by getting a dark dye job. My hair also used to be a lot longer. I wanted to change my appearance as quickly as possible, so the contact lenses are brown. I hope it looks convincing."

I'd love to see her as a blue-eyed blonde, even if she is spectacular as she is. I tell her, "Seems you've tried to think if everything to hide away from them. Won't you miss your family and friends, though?"

"Maybe, but I wasn't all that close to anyone after leaving college, and my job was awful, so this town is a breath of fresh air. As I said, I hadn't looked really hard for acting jobs, so I was working as a barista in a place where the customers were snooty and horrible. In comparison, Honeybee Hollow is like heaven, and the idea of essentially being sold into a marriage I don't want is disgusting. I would stay incognito the rest of my life to avoid it. I want to change my name legally, but I'm worried someone could find me because of that." She frowns. "We can't let anyone know around here, Blake. I don't want to put anyone else in danger from Sal. And I sure don't want to be ratted out to him so he can drag me back to New York."

I think about this for a moment and say, "I'm not so sure that's the right tactic. We may want to let folks know that there might be someone asking around about you, and they need to let me know right away. You could have the protection of the entire town that way. They don't need to know it's possibly the Mafia that's after you. We could say you're a stage actress from New York and you need a respite from the paparazzi or something. The downside of this idea is that someone might get anxious to sell you out for cash, and they also might start paying too much attention to you. These folks are great, but you never know how they'll react to the prospect of some serious money or living around a celebrity. I will have to alert the deputies in my office, but one person you need to tell all of this to is Juni. She needs to know there is possibly some danger in housing you over her business. It's only fair."

"Yeah, I see your point about Juni. She's been so great; I hate lying to her."

"What did you do with that piece of paper that said Honeybee Hollow on it?"

"I'm sorry to say I left it in my dresser at my parents' place. I had no reason to take it or destroy it when I ran across it, although now I know it might be a liability if someone finds it. But it's just a silly little scribble written by a kid with a pink marker. If anyone sees it, hopefully they would think it was nothing."

"Possibly, but we can't ignore it. Did you bring a computer with you? An IP address is one way people get located pretty easily."

"No. I had one, but I copied some personal stuff onto my new phone, wiped the hard drive clean, and then sold it. I worried about that too, even though it was a tough thing to ditch. I'm not using my old email address or anything that could link me to my former life in New York."

I nod at her, thankful she's covered her tracks pretty well

except for that damn little note. "You need to take care of that pile of money, Sloane. It's not safe, keeping it stashed like this. Why didn't you put it into the bank?"

"Partly because I didn't have time at first, and it was the weekend, but mostly because I was afraid to do anything besides stick it into a safe deposit box. I don't want to be discovered because I suddenly have a bank account in Kentucky."

"I get it. But the bank isn't going to expose you if you open a proper account; that's unconstitutional. And a checking account would be a lot more convenient than a safe deposit box. You can get a debit card from the bank to use in lieu of a credit card. There will be some federal forms to fill out for having a large amount of cash, but that still won't tip off Sal in any way. I'll be glad to escort you over there in the morning."

She looks at me with so much trust in her eyes, I'm suddenly too warm. But then she says, "Alright. We'll take it over there in the morning. What should we do until then?" She snuggles into my chest, giving me all kinds of ideas, and I'm a goner.

CHAPTER
Twelve

Sloane

I GUESS THE TIME FOR STORYTELLING AND OPENING UP IS over, and it's time to get to know one another in a different way. I try to convey my acceptance and eagerness by plastering myself against Blake's solid chest and nuzzling his neck. His hand gently nudges my face up so he can seal his lips over mine. This kiss is different from last night. He doesn't seem quite as desperate or needy—more confident and… can a kiss feel happy? It sure does to me, even after I've unloaded my bizarre situation on him. It must have blown his mind at least a little to learn some dude in the Mafia may be looking for me and wants to suck me into his criminal lifestyle. I'm sure Sal is furious, and my father is as well. But now's not the time to think about them. I wipe my mind clear and relish the feel of Blake's kisses.

I disengage myself momentarily so I can sit on his lap facing him. His eyes light up, and he smiles as I press myself against the generous hardness in his pants. I'm in no hurry, but I return his kisses with gusto as I enjoy his large hands stroking my arms, my back, and down to my butt. He grabs a handful and squeezes playfully as I grind against him.

"Sloane, you're doing all kinds of things to me, and I don't know if you're ready for the repercussions," he growls at me. "But I need to tell you that you are the most intriguing woman I've ever known, and I'm dying to see more of you… and to *do* more things to you."

"Bring it on, Sheriff. I'm ready," I pledge as I snake my hands under his shirt and relish the feel of his steely muscles and velvety skin. He has just the right amount of chest hair, I discover. It's soft and silky beneath my hands, and I want to rub my face in it. "Raise up your arms." He does, and I shove his shirt off, delighting in the sight of his lean physique. His muscles are beautifully chiseled without being too bulky. The sight of his perfect definition and gorgeous veined arms makes me squirm a little more on him.

"You too, beautiful. Your turn."

I respond by flinging my top off and tossing it to the floor. His eyes go immediately to my breasts, and I thank heaven I'm wearing pretty lingerie today. He buries his face in them with a small groan, muttering, "Magnificent."

"Blake?" I ask with a smile.

"Hmm?"

"Promise me you'll never call me baby?"

"You got it, sugar lump."

"Hmm…"

"Okay, I'll work on that."

"For now, just kiss me some more."

He raises an eyebrow. "Just kiss?"

"Maybe more than kissing. Please."

"Since you ask so nicely." He latches his mouth onto my breast and gently bites my nipple, making me gasp and squirm even more. I feel his hand go behind me where he deftly unhooks my bra, so I cooperate by shucking it off and tossing it on top of my shirt. "Yes," he says reverently. "So perfect."

"Please tell me you have a condom, Blake." I'm suddenly dying to get closer to this man, and when I say closer, I mean I want to feel him inside and out. I want him to fill me up, but not with a baby.

"I do." He grins and lifts me off his lap. He carries me the few feet to the bed where he gently deposits me, then reaches for his wallet. The sight of the foil packet he produces zings a thrill through me.

"Did you pack that just for me?"

He laughs. "I wasn't sure the kind of mood I'd find you in, but it's never wrong to be ready for anything." I notice he doesn't actually answer my question, but I don't really care. I'm just glad he's prepared.

I kick off my shoes and lie back on the bed, anxious to feel every inch of him. He's busy getting rid of his boots and socks, though, so I have to content myself with simply looking at him for a moment. "Do you work out a lot? You're pretty ripped."

"I exercise and run sometimes, but mostly I guess this is from heavy manual labor. I bought a run-down old mess of a house when I moved here, and fixing it up has been a back-breaking work in progress. It's looking pretty great though, so it's been worth it."

"I'd love to see it."

"And I'd love to show it to you. Later." He stands and turns toward me. "Now, undo your jeans, beautiful. There are other things I want to see today."

I do, and he whisks my pants off. Now I'm just in my panties, and they aren't concealing much of anything. His eyes sparkle as he looks at me. Immediately, he shucks his jeans, only his boxers also come off just as quickly. And… oh my. Now *that's* what I call a love muscle—or maybe a club. Long and thick with glorious veins and a shiny dot of precum announcing how ready he is to fuck me. I stare at his dick and lick my lips, making him groan.

"See something you want, darlin'?" he asks with a cocky grin, and I nod greedily.

I didn't tell Blake that when Sal asked me to go to bed with him, he grabbed my hand and held it to his crotch. He may have been hard, but there wasn't anything impressive about what I felt—not that I wanted a thing to do with the man for *any* reason. I banish this thought as soon as it creeps unbidden into my head. Instead, I raise up, slip my panties off, and reach for Blake. A shudder runs through him as I wrap my hand firmly around his girth and lick the precum from his tip. "Mmm."

I slide what I can manage into my mouth, and Blakes starts swearing under his breath. He sounds pretty happy despite his choice of words, so I consider his reaction encouragement and start to give him my all.

"God, I adore a woman who can suck dick. Sloane, you're amazing." I'm using my tongue and teeth on him, noting his reactions with each new movement. He seems to especially love having my teeth scrape him. I know some guys hate that, but those who like it get off on it. Not that I've had dozens of lovers or anything, but I've done my research. I give him a long, hard pull, sucking him deep, when he pats my cheek and tells me in a strained voice, "I think you better quit for now, sweet stuff. I don't want this to be over too quickly; you're too good at it." His legs are shaking a bit, so I understand. Sure was fun though.

"My turn," he tells me. "I love to *eat*, as I've mentioned. Now lie back and open your legs wide." I comply with no embarrassment at all. This man is looking at me like I'm incredibly beautiful to him, and I can barely take it. "Ohh, look at that. You're so pink and pretty," he says as he gently draws his finger through my dampness. He circles around my clit, eliciting a soft moan of encouragement from me, but instead of lingering, he shoves his finger inside.

I gasp with the sudden invasion as he begins to stroke in and out, curling his finger so that it rubs against my G-spot. Like everything about this man, his hands are large and strong… and he's unpredictable. His other hand goes to my breast where he plays with my nipple a moment before giving it a strong pinch. Again, I suck in my breath and feel my pussy clench around him, getting wetter and wetter by the moment. "Ohmygawd," I breathe. "Do that again." He laughs softly, and just as I think he's not going to do it, *wham*. He's not even touching my clit, but I'm a hair's breadth away from having an orgasm, I swear.

Blake leans down and finally strokes my clit gently with his tongue. I start to shake and feel my climax beginning. It's inevitable now. But when he sucks my clit into his mouth and lashes me with his stiff tongue, I explode like Vesuvius.

"*Blake*," I cry, "*yes!*" Hot waves of lava course through my veins as I clench his finger—or is that two fingers now? I can't even remember him changing it up. All I know is that exquisite pleasure engulfs me. I shudder and quake with unbelievable sensations. The feelings go on and on as he laps at me until I can barely breathe. He pulls back, and I watch through blissed-out eyes as he rips the condom package open with his teeth and rolls it on. *Sexy!* I can't wait.

Instead of simply impaling me, Blake lies down on the bed

and tells me, "I'd love to watch you ride me, Sloane. You control this. Do whatever you want."

So, with an eager smile, I climb over him and slide myself slowly and carefully down onto him. If he felt big in my mouth, it's nothing to the way he feels in my pussy. He's probably learned that some women might be intimidated by his size. But to me, I love the slight burn and the tremendous sense of fullness as I engulf him inch by inch. Once I have him in all the way, I smile and whisper, "I've never felt anything so perfect in my life."

I begin to rise up and down on him, and he reaches for me so he can continue to stroke my clit. I squeeze him with my inner muscles, and he groans with pleasure, but I'm getting so lost in my own bliss, I lose the rhythm a little. This doesn't seem to bother Blake as he speeds up his manipulations on my clit, and I'm off again into another orgasm, just as fantastic as the first one. He then grabs me by the hips and rams me up and down on him several times until he lets out a colossal moan, and his eyes close. Once more, he thrusts upward into me mightily, and I feel him unloose everything into me. It's a beautiful sight watching this man in the throes of ecstasy.

When we're both done quivering and shuddering, Blake gently lifts me off of him and positions me next to him in the bed. "Be right back," he tells me, and I sigh, admiring his muscled backside as he heads to the bathroom. He's back quickly with a warm washcloth. Such a considerate lover.

Since it's getting chilly in the room—or maybe it was

before, and we didn't notice—we climb under the covers, and I snuggle into his embrace as he cocoons me with his strong arms, turning me into the little spoon.

"Blake," I say softly, "I sure am glad you showed up today."

"Me too, sugar lips. This was the best day I've had in years. Or maybe ever." I can't help giggling a little at his endearment, but he stops me by asking, "May I take you out to dinner later?"

"Um, sure. Thanks. Where do you want to go?"

"Are you ready to discover the best burger in the world? I'd like to introduce you to Sock Hop. It's a local institution, and you haven't fully experienced Honeybee Hollow until you've sampled their fine cuisine."

"Sounds like fun. Do you mind if I close my eyes for a little while first? I didn't get a lot of sleep last night, and I'm pretty tired."

"I was going to recommend that, honey." He sounds sleepy to me too.

"Blake?"

"Hmm?"

"So far, I think I like darlin' the best, but you can keep trying."

"Sure thing, *mi corazón*." He gives me a gentle squeeze, and we both drift off. My last conscious thought is that the feel of all this naked flesh is incredibly delicious.

CHAPTER

Thirteen

SOMETHING IS RUBBING MY DICK, AND IT FEELS LIKE HEAVEN. I slowly wake and remember my surroundings. I'm in bed with the most exquisite woman I've even known, and she's buffing my boner with her delightful backside. "Troublemaker," I grumble with way more laughter than anger in my voice. I reach down and squeeze a big handful of her butt cheek. "Keep it up, and I may just have to fuck this naughty bottom of yours."

"Mmm, yes please, Sheriff. Maybe you can handcuff me when you do it."

Is she for real? I sit up. "Seriously, Sloane?" Now's not the time for joking around. We've only had sex one time, and she's already up for a little kink—and butt play?

She flips over and looks me in the eye. "I somehow get the feeling that you're an adventurous lover, and I want to try everything you like. I honestly don't have all that much experience, but I'm willing."

I clear my throat, and my voice cracks a bit when I say, "Well, okay then. We'll explore things together." But my stomach lets out a mighty rumble, and Sloane gets the giggles.

"You really do need to eat a lot, don't you?"

"Sadly, yes. It's a curse. Oh, and I don't have any more condoms."

"Well, then let's go take a quick shower and get your hollow leg filled."

"Would you like to come back to my place after dinner?" I draw a circle around her nipple and grin as it perks right up under my touch. "We can have a sleepover, and I have lots of condoms there."

Looking pleased, she says, "That sounds great. I have Mondays off, so I can definitely go to your house and then to the bank in the morning."

"Then pack your toothbrush and whatever you'll need, and we'll take care of your business in the morning."

Laughing, she pulls me off the bed and leads me by the hand to the shower.

Fourteen

SLOANE

IT TURNS OUT SOCK HOP IS EVERYTHING IT'S CRACKED UP TO be. Poodle skirts, servers on roller skates, and cool fifties décor with a checkered tile floor. The menu is basic—consisting mostly of burgers, fries, and milkshakes, but they have an interesting variety of options to dress the burgers up—everything from good old American chili to French truffles and fresh rings of pineapple. But the Sock Hop special—and the most popular meal on the menu—is a fully loaded cheeseburger with a huge pile of fries and a shake. An old-fashioned jukebox plays fifties hits that make me want to get up and dance. It's perfect, and we luckily snag a booth where we can sit next to one another before the place fills up. By the time we order, it's packed in here.

Blake and I attract a lot of attention from the other diners. There are plenty of cocked eyebrows and not-so-carefully concealed thumbs-up gestures directed at Blake. He just smiles benignly back at them. I'm getting a lot of jealous looks from the female population though, and it makes me wonder how many hearts he's broken in this town, so I ask him quietly, "Why is everyone staring at us, and how many of these ladies have you scorned? I'm getting more than my share of the evil eye."

"Don't let them get to you, cupcake. They're staring because you're new and you're gorgeous. Please understand, though, I have never let myself date a single soul in this town. I purposely stayed clear of any of the residents so I wouldn't end up with someone having hurt feelings who'd end up running into me over and over. They're just jealous for their own dumb reasons. I promise you no one *knows me* like you do."

"So you broke your self-imposed rule for me? Why?"

"Because, sugar pie, I never met anyone worth breaking my rule for before. After meeting you, I couldn't resist you no matter how hard I tried." He lowers his voice so only I can hear him, "And now that I've tasted your sweetness, I might have to turn into your love slave."

I snort out a laugh and bop his shoulder playfully. "Sure, sure. I'm irresistible."

"You are. And now that we've been spotted all cozied up together, the message has been delivered."

"So coming to Sock Hop was a strategic move? I thought you were introducing me to the local culture." I can't be mad at him; he's just too damn cute.

"Two birds, one stone." He leans in and kisses me, and I swear I hear a few feminine gasps from around us. He tries to make it a quick one, but my arms go around him, and I scooch closer.

"Are we making a scene?" I whisper finally when he comes up for air.

"Do you know how many teenagers have made out in this place over the past few decades? The regular patrons are used to some kissing."

"But we're adults."

"Then this is just our warm-up for later," he says, nuzzling my neck.

We pull apart when a waitress places our enormous burger dinners in front of us. "So much food!" I gasp. Then I notice the waitress standing there sort of shimmying her booty and waiting for Blake to take notice.

"Necessary fuel for nighttime games," he tells me with a wink, totally ignoring her.

"Can I get you anything else?" she asks in a breathy voice.

Blake shakes his head, not looking at her, and says dismissively, "We're good, thanks."

Her shoulders droop as she skates away.

Not wanting to be in a food coma, and sufficiently stuffed, I quit way before Blake finishes eating. But when I notice him eyeballing the leftover portion of my dinner, I shove the plate toward him. He grins and polishes it all off. The man must have the metabolism of a hummingbird.

As soon as we're done, Blake takes care of the check. On our way toward the door, our waitress skates by us again, trying to catch Blake's eye. Blake misses it because he was reaching to open the door for me, but I smile at her. She gives me a sour look and skates off. I'm privately pleased Blake doesn't seem to realize she's alive, especially considering how cute she is.

My curiosity gets the better of me as we drive to his house, so I ask, "Our waitress tonight seemed a little fixated on you. Did you ever date her?"

He gets a perplexed look on his face and asks, "Not if she's from around here. What did she look like?"

"Blonde, perky, pretty. Her nametag said Crystal." Obviously, she didn't make much of an impression on him even though she tried her best.

"Doesn't ring a bell, so I'd say definitely not. Like I told you, I've stayed away from women who live here."

End of discussion, apparently.

I can't wait to see Blake's house. He mentioned it with pride, so I'm anxious to see his handiwork. It sits way back from a narrow road on a large, wooded lot. I imagine the forest is gorgeous when the leaves are fully out. He has what looks like a single-story log cabin that sprawls in various directions as if the original owner kept having a larger and larger family and needed to add on. The doors, windows, porch, and the trim are obviously all new, but they still manage to blend in well with the original timbers of the house.

"Come on in, and I'll give you the grand tour," he says with unconcealed pride.

The outside is picturesque, but the inside is a work of art. It seems he took down walls and joined smaller rooms together to make larger living areas, but each space is oddly shaped due to the original configurations. The lack of square spaces adds to the charm of the house. There are multiple bookshelves positioned around the space, and I can't wait to see what Blake reads. The floor is rustic hardwood panels polished to a high sheen and covered in woven rugs. I can see two natural stone fireplaces—one in the kitchen area and one in the larger great room. Several of the tables seem to be home-crafted by someone with a lot of talent and great imagination.

"You did all of this yourself?"

"Most of it. The plumbing, gas, and electric work were all updated by the pros, but I did whatever I could myself. I'm still not finished."

"How did you learn to do this? Did you learn woodworking in the Marines or something?"

Blake bursts out laughing. "Far from it. No, I watched hours and hours of YouTube videos. You can learn how to build furniture, upholster old chairs, install insulation—all kinds of things." He looks thoughtful for a minute and adds, "You know who's really great at this kind of stuff?"

"Who?"

"Juni's man Asher Bellamy. He designed a lot of the house we went to the other night. Too bad you didn't see more of his work, but I'm sure you'll see it all sometime."

"There certainly are some talented people in this little town."

"Just another thing adding to its charm. Now… are you ready to see the bedroom?"

"You bet," I say with a wink. He takes me by the hand, picks up my overnight bag in his other hand, and leads me down a hall. Looking around, I tell him, "Blake, you're missing something here."

"What?"

"You need a dog."

"Indeed I do. It's on my list, but it has to be the right one. I have to have a companion who doesn't mind a little police work and who'd be happy with me at the office and accompanying me in the patrol car. But he also needs to be a calm house dog."

"I love dogs, but I've never had one."

"A couple of the foster families I lived with had dogs, and that was always the best part of living there. I was always sad to leave them when I got traded in for a better kid."

Blake makes light of his situation, but I can imagine how

hurt he must have felt being rejected repeatedly. It's a wonder he can relate to people at all after being so poorly cared for. I blurt out a question that is probably none of my business at this point in our budding relationship: "Blake, do you ever want to have children?"

He eyes me a moment and answers solemnly, "In theory anyway, I've always craved having a family, and I'd love nothing more than three or four kids. But in truth, I don't know what kind of a father I'd make—or a husband either for that matter. I never had a father, and I don't remember having a mother or a grandmother. I've never seen a healthy relationship up close, and the one serious one I tried to have ended up in shambles. My foster parents rarely, if ever, showed affection, so I don't know if that's stunted me, or if I'd be able to figure things out on my own. The type of home life I experienced always seemed more transactional than domestic. I know real families aren't the idealized versions you see in movies or on TV where everyone is all perfect and loving, but there has to be more than what I lived through. I hope I'm not scaring you away." He sits on the edge of the bed and pats the spot next to him, so I sit down beside him.

Choosing my words carefully, I tell Blake, "My life is too complicated to expect you to devote yourself to me in a serious relationship right away, so I certainly have no expectations. But I'm incredibly drawn to you, and I'd love to explore what we can mean to one another by taking what we have day by day. You're a kind man, and that is so attractive. You make me feel safe, which is something I haven't felt… well, possibly ever. From the little I know about you so far, I'd say you'd figure out how to parent with the best of 'em. The biggest motivator must be caring enough to do your best, don't you think?"

He nods thoughtfully, so I continue, "As we've discussed, you do seem to run a little hot and cold, so you're not too predictable, but that may have just been because of the doubts you had about me—and for solid reasons. I know I blew into town with an incredible amount of baggage, and I'm not talking about the bag of money. I could possibly be a threat to the tranquility of this wonderful town. I hope I don't disrupt lives, but there's a chance. As the town sheriff who's responsible for everyone's welfare, you might have to tell me to move along, and I'll do so to protect you and the friends I've already made here." I clasp his hand in mine and ask, "Can we try this—whatever it is between us—and see how it goes? It may all blow up, or maybe it'll turn into the fairytale happy ever after we both want."

CHAPTER
Fifteen

BLAKE

I blow out a breath. "You're amazing, Sloane. I'm sorry I've jerked you around, and I'll try not to do it anymore. Also, I won't give you any more feeble excuses like when I said I was getting too turned on and then left you standing there wondering about my sanity. What I do is probably a self-preservation tactic when I see something I want badly and don't feel worthy enough to have." She scoffs at me. "No, seriously. Not to be sappy or cliché, but you're like a breath of fresh air in my life suddenly, and I can't get enough, but I'm scared to death you'll wake up and realize I'm not worth the trouble." I nuzzle her neck and delight in the goosebumps that pop up on her arms. I love the reaction I elicit from her. "I'm done talking for a while," I whisper into her ear. "I desperately need to fuck you senseless now."

"Fine by me," she tells me and pulls me even closer.

In less than a minute, our clothes have disappeared, but it's terribly chilly in this room. I leave her a moment and light the bedroom fireplace. I also turn out the lights and take in her beauty in the flickering firelight. I drag a row of condoms out of the bedside drawer, then a thought crosses my mind, so I ask, "How do *you* feel about children?"

"At the moment, I don't want to think about them, but in general, I'd love to have some, if and when I can get my life on track. Now let's get back to fucking me senseless, okay, Sheriff?"

"Absolutely, snuggle bunny."

"Oh, no. Not that one," she giggles.

Over the next hour or two (I'm not wasting my time looking at the clock), I plan to wring several lovely orgasms out of my delightful woman. I may not want to spook her away by saying it, but I know in my heart Sloane is mine. Mine to keep and mine to love. It's way too soon to lay that on her, and I'm no idiot, so I keep those thoughts to myself. I do keep her happy, though, by kissing and stroking every glorious inch of her. I gorge myself looking at her delicious body. Those tits that feel just right in my hands with those nipples that respond so quickly to my lips and fingers. She has a fabulous ass that is toned and round, and I want to spank it so that it turns red before I plow into it. The very thought makes my dick weep with precum.

She's a generous lover and unashamed of her body, which she uses and gives to me unselfishly. She obviously loves it when I suck on her clit and probe her with both hands at the same time. She reacts so well to that, after fucking her sweet pussy a couple of times, I lube up her ass and show her how exciting that can be. I'm careful with her, taking things slowly—and skip the spanking part for now—but when I'm finally balls-deep in her backside and stroking her clit, she hollers, "Faster, harder, Blake. Fuck me now!" I know I've found a winner. I come so hard I think my head—or maybe it's my heart—will explode. We collapse in a heap after that and only rouse ourselves long enough to take a quick shower.

Sloane removes her brown contact lenses to go to bed, and a jolt goes through me when I look for the first time into her lovely *blue* eyes instead of the fake brown ones. It's as if the final veil has been lifted—and just for me. From now on, I hope she will get rid of the lenses before we make love. I'll have to remember to ask.

Sloane is asleep in my arms, and I'm exhausted in the best way, but I'm also imagining what a life with this woman might be like over the long haul. I am such a sap, I start to think up names for kids and then tell myself to fucking go to sleep.

I have it bad for this woman.

EARLY THE NEXT MORNING, I DROP HER BACK AT HER PLACE and check on things in the sheriff's office until the bank is about to open. Nothing of great interest is going on except that Sheriff Hansen's funeral has been scheduled, so I do some paperwork until I know we can get into the bank. I head back to Sloane's and find her trying to unstick the zipper on that darn gym bag. I can tell she's frustrated, so I ask, "Do you think there might be a candle in a kitchen drawer or cupboard?"

"Um, possibly," she answers and lets go of the bag. She rummages around until she finds a candle in the back of a utensil drawer. I show her how to rub it all over the teeth of the zipper, and poof! It slides up and down like nothing was ever wrong with it. Sloane looks so pleased she bestows a scorching kiss on me. I'm suddenly fantasizing about climbing into her bed, but she laughs and says, "Come on, hot stuff. Let's get to the bank."

I smile broadly because she's way better at pet names than I am.

When we arrive, the tellers are already busy with a few customers. Knowing what Sloane needs to do is making me uncomfortable, so I lead her to the back of the bank and locate the manager. "Hiram, Sloane here needs to conduct some banking business that requires some privacy. Do you think you could take care of it in your office? And close the door?" The idea of sitting out there and counting out well over a hundred thousand dollars cash in broad daylight gives me the heebie-jeebies.

He's all smiles and stands to greet us. "Mornin', Blake. Certainly, I'd be happy to assist this young lady." He sticks out his hand and introduces himself. "I understand you're new to our lovely town. And I hear our Sheriff Ogden is taking fine care of you."

I try not to roll my eyes while Sloane turns pink. I turn to her and ask, "Do you want me to stay, or would you rather take care of this on your own?"

"Oh, no, please stay, Blake." She looks nervous. Thinking she might be afraid that he'll distrust her, I lead her to Hiram's desk and pull out a chair for her, sit down beside her, and set the bag on the floor between us.

The transaction takes way longer than I'd hoped, but eventually she has an interest-bearing checking account, a couple of CDs, and a debit card. She had way more money in that thing than I expected. Good lord. I had no idea how much a barely used Maserati could bring in, and the jewelry must have been incredibly expensive stuff. I can well imagine that Sal Caputo is awfully steamed right now since his monetary investment in Sloane didn't appeal to her any more than his romantic advances did. I hope for Sloane's sake the jewelry was purchased legitimately, but I have no way of knowing. Anyway, the responsibility was on whoever bought it from her to make sure it wasn't stolen.

The last item of business I have is to tell Hiram, "Please keep this transaction with Sloane confidential. I can assure you that she's on the up and up, but there may be some interest in her whereabouts from someone we'd rather not alert. We're trusting you, Hiram. This is a delicate matter. And if anyone strange comes snooping around asking questions, please let me know immediately."

"Absolutely understood. Our policy is complete privacy for our customers. It goes without saying. It's been a pleasure doing business with you, and if you have any questions or special needs from here on out, here's my card." He hands it to Sloane. He looks way more professional and concerned than he did when we walked in with that ratty bag.

When we head back outside, I ask Sloane, "Ready for some lunch? I'm starving. And they have a great lunch buffet on Mondays at the Honeybee Hollow Inn."

"Lead the way, handsome."

I lean over and whisper in her ear, "Thanks, but I prefer 'hot stuff.'"

"Of course you do," she says with a wink.

After we fill our plates with all kinds of delicious items and sit back down at our table by the window, I quietly ask Sloane, "Did you by any chance save a photo of Sal when you got your new phone?"

Shaking her head, she tells me, "He never wanted to have

a picture taken. But I was so grossed out by him by the time I left, I never would have saved one even if I'd had one. Sorry. I know it would be helpful."

"Can you describe him for me?"

"Sure. He's about five eleven, broad shoulders, dark brown hair, brown eyes, and clean shaven. He wears a diamond in one ear—I forget which one—and he has really bright white teeth that look like they've been bleached too much. Oh, and he has a small but jagged scar on his chin like maybe someone socked him wearing a ring or something. I always wondered how he got it, but I never asked. He dresses well and keeps his hair neat and trimmed. Basically, he's fairly handsome but pretty nondescript."

"Okay, that helps."

After we finish our lunch, I introduce Sloane to the owner of the inn and tell her, "If a dark-haired, average-sized guy who sounds like a Yankee shows up and starts asking any questions that seem odd, please lie through your teeth to him and call me immediately. He wears a diamond earring and has a small scar on his chin. He might need a room for the night, and I'd appreciate it if you let me know. Don't give him any information about newcomers to town or anything like that. Can you do that for me, Betty?"

"Absolutely, Sheriff. Oh, it sounds so good calling you that, Blake. We're all so thankful for you in this town." She beams at me like a proud mama, and I blush. "And good luck to the two of you, I'm happy to have met you finally, Sloane.

You're just as pretty as everyone says and just what our young man here needs." Now it's Sloane's turn to blush.

I swear, the people in this town…

"One more thing, Betty. Please keep this conversation to yourself, okay?" I doubt she will, but I can try.

"You bet, Sheriff."

As we head out the door, I fully expect her to be on the phone already with one of her cronies saying, "This is a secret, so don't spread it around. I'm just telling you… blah, blah, blah."

"Another strategic meal, Blake?" Sloane asks me, breaking me out of my reverie.

"Sort of. I was hungry, you needed to eat too, and Betty has the best accommodations in town—besides a couple of the bed and breakfast places. I don't see your former boyfriend showing up and wanting to stay in one of those, however. He's probably not too interested in historic Kentucky homes."

"He was never my boyfriend."

"Didn't you wear his ring?"

"Only as long as I had to in order to avoid suspicion. Yuck."

"I know, bad joke." I swing my arm around her shoulders. "Look, I have to get back to the office now, but I sure want to see you tonight. Can you make it over to my place so I can make dinner for you and then burn it off again?"

"I can't wait," she says with a longing look. "In the meantime, I need to call Juni and have that chat with her. I don't want to wait for tomorrow and have to do it while we're up to our eyeballs with customers."

"Good thinking." I give her a quick kiss, eliciting a catcall from someone across the street. We're right in front of Hot Stuff, so I know Sloane doesn't have far to go to get home. I reluctantly head for my office, sorry to have to get back to my job instead of enjoying her company. I have it so bad for her I wonder how I'm going to make it through the afternoon without her.

OVER THE NEXT COUPLE OF WEEKS, I FIND MYSELF FALLING deeper and deeper in love with this incredible woman. She's funny, charming, brave enough to take me on, and willing to try anything. She actually asked me one night if I'd try spanking her, and I thought I'd cream my boxers before getting them off. I took it easy on her, so it was just as much fun as I'd hoped, and Sloane loved it. Her cheeks got all pink and rosy, and I had to kiss them to make them better. I thought she was going to pass out when she came.

I can't get enough of Sloane, and I love eating her out like she's my favorite candy. Speaking of that, a couple of years ago one of my hookups asked me if she tasted sweet enough for me, but when I looked at her like she was crazy, she was incensed. We had a very confusing conversation after that, but

I came away with the knowledge that women who read idealized romance books are led to believe that their "nectar" is sweet. Hah! What a disservice to women. A pussy tastes like a pussy, and some lovers (like yours truly) embrace the flavor, while others aren't so fond of it. Sloane isn't sweet either. She's musky and delicious, and just right. I could spend hours between her legs.

On top of being a fantastic girlfriend (because I've started introducing her that way, and she hasn't objected), Sloane has started researching dogs for me like she's getting a master's degree in canine behavior. I'm sure life has never been so great.

Then I get a strange call from Betty.

CHAPTER
Sixteen

SALVATORE CAPUTO

New York, a couple of weeks ago.

HOW DARE THAT FUCKING BITCH IGNORE MY CALLS! WHY isn't she answering me? Am I gonna hafta go over to that armpit of an apartment she calls home and slap some sense into her? She's mine, goddammit. *I make the rules.* Nobody ignores Sal Caputo!

I beat it over to Anna's place and don't see the Maserati anywhere. Just fucking great. I wonder where she's gone—not to work, for sure. I ordered her to quit that stupid job because I'd be taking care of her from here on out. Luckily, I made sure there was a tracker in the car. I hadn't expected to need to find her because the chick is clearly hot for me. She proved that the other night when she was practically in tears about not being able to fuck. I almost gave her the thrill of sucking my dick before I headed out, but I was afraid she'd get too carried away and need to get it on for real, and I can't stand it when chicks are on the rag, so I wasn't going there. I'm glad she warned me at least. Nothin's worse than finding out that shit by surprise.

Well, the car's not here, so I check the finder app and… what the fuck? What is that crazy bitch doing in Philly? Does she have some secret boyfriend? I'll kill the bastard if he's touching my fiancée! Or… did she let the car get stolen or something? I look up the address, and what I discover makes me so mad I'm about to have a heart attack. She's taken the MC20 to a Maserati dealership. I would wonder if the car had a problem, but no one would go all the way down there to have it serviced when we have places lots closer. It also occurs to me, though, that maybe someone else took the car to Philly. Too many possibilities. Something's up, and I don't like the smell of it one bit.

I call the dealership and ask them if they know anything about a Maserati MC20 being brought in for service or trade-in by a young woman. The bitch on the phone says she has no way of knowing that information but assures me they have a couple of them for sale if I'd like to come in and see them. When I ask her what color they are, she says she thinks they're both blue. She won't quote any prices or give me any more information than that. The one I gave Anna was blue, but so are plenty of 'em out there. I thought it was a romantic gesture, seeing as how she has blue eyes.

I get out of my car and go up to Anna's apartment, ready to wring her neck if she's there. But the door is wide open, and out comes some shady dude carrying bags of stuff. Is he robbing her? I need to protect her! I storm up to the guy and ask, "What do you think you're doin'?" as I grab him by his shirt.

"Let go a me!" he almost spits in my face. I wonder if the guy's ever met a toothbrush or a bottle of mouthwash. Phew! "My ex-tenant left a buncha junk in her apartment when she left, and I'm clearin' it out."

"She's *gone*? Gone where?"

"How the hell should I know? She sent me a text that she was leavin', and that was all. Now get outta my way so I can finish this job and find a new tenant. Money don't grow on trees. Know what I'm sayin'?"

"Can I look around in there?"

"Are you lookin' to rent?"

"Uh…"

"Get the fuck outta here."

She probably cleared out all of the expensive shit I gave her anyway, so I don't know what I'd find that would be valuable information. I decide to leave. This place is such a dump, it's giving me an itch.

It's time to check with Daddy and Mommy to see what they know about their precious Anna. They got me into this with her in the first place. Her dad sang her praises like a songbird. She was supposedly beautiful (he proved that with a photo) and so respectful she'd make the perfect wife. As soon as I laid eyes on her I knew her looks and sophistication would help me look reputable to people I need to impress. She seemed obedient and definitely not as smart as me—the perfect blonde wife. Now I wonder if it was all an act.

I bet she got wind of her dad's debts and sold the car to get her dad out of trouble. Well, that sacrifice was for nothing. That sucker needs a lot more than what that car's worth, and my business plan is going to make us both rich if she'll just hold up her end of the bargain. I need her father's loyalty, and marrying her will both guarantee that and protect me from her ever testifying against me if shit goes down the wrong way. If we don't marry, I'll have to find someone else to do business with. I sure do want to get a load of her gorgeous mouth around my dick in the worst way though. Apparently, I need to fuck some sense into her. One taste of me, and she'll fall into line. I'm great with the ladies—ask anyone.

I show up at Hank and Minnie Sloane's place unannounced at dinnertime, expecting to find all three of them. On the trip over, I decided Anna was smart to get rid of that dumpy apartment and move back home until we're married, so I'm a little shocked to find that Anna's not here with them. Where the hell is she? They look happy to see me and set an extra place for me, so I sit down to some really mediocre pasta. If I were a nice guy, I'd ask my ma to give them her recipe. I think this crap came out of a box, and the sauce is watery and boring.

Anyway, I take a big swallow of barely drinkable wine and ask, "So, where's Anna?" I've been here several times before on my own, so I guess that's why they didn't ask me first why she wasn't with me.

Her mom looks blank, and her dad answers, "No idea. Did you call her?"

"I tried. She's not answering."

"Really?" Minnie says with a surprised look. She looks nervously at her husband. "I wonder why not. I haven't spoken to her in days."

"Don't you speak to your own daughter every day?" What kind of parents are these people? My ma calls me all the time. When Minnie looks shocked, I add, "Then you might not know that she's not at home at that piss pot apartment where she lived on accounta she's moved out, and her new car is at some dealership in Philly."

"What?" her dad asks. He does look genuinely alarmed.

"So she's not trying to pay off your debts by getting rid of her wedding gift from me?"

"Of course not. She has no idea about my financial… situation." He's not looking at me when he says this, so I'm not a hundred percent convinced.

Still, I hope he's telling me the truth because that makes me feel lots better and makes more sense to me. She's genuinely falling for me then. *I knew it.* The question remains though: Where is she?

"Humor me. Call your daughter and ask her what the hell is going on with her."

"I'll call her as soon as we're done eating," he says—as if he actually likes this so-called food.

"Call. Her. Now." I glare at him with the Caputo Eye. It never fails to strike fear in the hearts of lesser men.

"Uh, sure, Sal," Hank replies, pulling out his phone. He dials and waits. He waits and waits until her voice mail message clicks on, and he waits for that to finish. "Hi, Anna… honey. Call me. This is your dad, and I need to talk to you right away." Of course it's her dad. Doesn't this jerk understand she can see his number? And wouldn't she recognize his voice? "I'll try again after dinner, Sal. Maybe she's out with friends in a noisy place, and she can't hear the phone ring or something."

So we make stupid-shit small talk about flowers, music, and other wedding crap while we have dessert and coffee. All the time I'm wondering how he eats this lousy grub. Is it all that low-fat garbage? There's no flavor in anything. This is nothing like the dinner they had when I met Anna. They musta been buttering me up—or had it catered. I'm gonna need a Tums after this meal. Finally, we get up from the table, and I follow Hank into his home office while his wife clears the dishes.

"Cigar? Brandy?" he offers, so of course I go for both. Gotta wash the taste of that food outta my mouth.

"Look, Hank, I sure as fuck hope there isn't any problem with our arrangement. But I have to say, I'm getting a bad feeling. Go ahead and try calling Anna again."

He punches in her number, and I wonder why he doesn't have her on speed dial. It rings once this time, and his face goes all pasty-looking as he listens to something on the other end of the call.

"Well, shit," he mumbles and looks at me with real concern this time. "Uh…"

"So what the fuck is it?"

"Her number is out of service."

"And you haven't seen her for days."

"No."

The wife wanders in just as I tell him, "I think she's been kidnapped."

Minnie gasps like she's having an attack of the vapors and clutches her heart, falling into a chair. She nearly screams at her husband, "Call the police!"

"*Do not* call the police," I tell him as he starts to dial 911. "I have a guy who can find anyone. Leave it to me. He's like a bloodhound, and he's never failed me yet." Noticing their worried expressions, I try to make them feel a little better. "Look, I'll be in touch soon, and you'll probably have a visit from my guy. Name's Damien. He'll have questions. He's really the best, I promise you. Be patient; he's very thorough. We'll just have to make sure he knows to bring her back alive."

CHAPTER

Seventeen

SALVATORE CAPUTO

I BEAT IT OUTTA THEIR HOUSE AND BACK TO MY CAR FOR A private conversation with my guy Damien. I've known him since we were in juvie together. He has an uncanny ability for finding people and taking care of them however he needs to. He's matured a lot since we were punks and has developed some special talents.

I call Damien and fill him in the best I can. He asks a bunch of questions and says he'll start by going through what's left of her apartment tonight—although he's pissed I waited this long to let him know. He never minds breaking in —especially crappy joints like her apartment building. The guy's like a genius. I also give him the information about the Maserati dealership. Maybe he can get more info out of them than that bitch gave me over the phone.

Did I mention that Damien is a handsome fucker? He can sweet-talk almost anyone into coughing up the deets. And if he can't do it with his looks and charm, he does it with muscle. He's not squeamish and has a creative imagination. I'm just glad we're friends. With the face of an angel, the physique of Thor, and the heart of Genghis Khan, he frankly scares the shit outta me. He'll also fuck *anyone* if it'll get him what he wants.

"Is there anything else Anna might have with her that someone would want to steal, or she may have hocked?"

This really makes my blood boil. She wouldn't do something like that. "Look, asshole, she was kidnapped. She loves me, and she wouldn't just get rid of her stuff like that. But, yeah, she has an engagement ring that cost me a shit-ton of money, some other fancy-ass jewelry, and stuff I bought her. No way she'd have hocked anything herself, but if someone stole it all from her, maybe they've hocked it and dumped her in a river somewhere." I feel like a sentimental jerk when my voice cracks with that last thought.

Damien just grunts at me. Then he asks about her parents and gets their contact info so he can go see them.

"Just don't go scaring them, okay? They're worried about their daughter, and they aren't too bright."

"Sure boss, I'll treat 'em with kid gloves and be on my best behavior. But did you consider that *they* might have hocked her stuff to pay off their debts and then sent her off to who-knows-where?"

Sighing, I say, "Yeah, it's occurred to me, but they were genuinely surprised and worried about her. They aren't good enough actors to pull that off, trust me."

"If you say so. I'll get on this tonight."

"Thanks, Dame."

He grunts at me again and says, "You know the price."

"Yeah, yeah. You'll have your cash."

I HAVE TO WAIT THREE FUCKING DAYS BEFORE I HEAR BACK from Damien, and I'm so nervous, I can barely handle my own affairs. I'm just sure someone captured Anna, stole everything from her, and then raped her before dumping her somewhere or selling her to someone. My imagination runs wild, and I can't sleep at night because I'm worrying so much. I should be better than this! I'm not in love with her... am I? Fucking hell, I *am* in love, and I gotta get my woman back!

The first information Damien calls me with is confusing. "I went down to Philly. The car you bought Anna is definitely the one that's at the dealership. It was brought in by a woman, but she didn't match Anna's description at all. So maybe whoever kidnapped her has a female accomplice. They refused to tell me anything else about the transaction, and I didn't think it was worth ruffling up any feathers over that.

"I can't believe you didn't have a photo of your own fiancée, Sal. I finally got one from her parents today when I went to see them. They're such dopes, though. The one they gave me is five years old, from when she graduated college. Don't these people give a shit about their own kid? They seemed worried, but the father was clearly more concerned about his association with you falling through than about his daughter."

"Sounds about right."

"They didn't give me much to work with, so I'm going to try to find more of the stuff you gave her and maybe establish a pattern or something. I have a sense that her mom and dad are too clueless to give me anything worthwhile. They don't know who her friends are, where she likes to go for fun… nothing. They couldn't even tell me where she worked—only that she waitressed or something."

"She was a barista."

"Where?"

"Dunno."

"Well, that gives me a lot to go on. You know how many places she might have worked in New York? Thousands! What's wrong with you? You're almost as self-absorbed as her parents."

"Hey! Don't give me any shit. Who pays attention to the names of coffee joints?"

"Do you want to find her or not?"

"Of course I do. Get to work and get off my back."

"I'm gonna need a miracle finding this one. The price just doubled."

"Fuck you, Damien."

"You too, Sal."

"Let me know when you find her."

"What's the magic word?"

"Fucking let me know when you find her, *please*. Oh, and… uh… I don't think she'd ever get rid of it, but I'm going to send you a photo of the receipt I got from buying her engagement ring. It has a picture of the ring on the receipt."

"You didn't think that was important until now?"

"No."

The asshole has the balls to laugh at me. But now I have a sinking feeling because I also gave Anna a copy of it. I didn't want her thinking I'd bought some stupid cubic zirconia or something.

"Dame?"

"Yeah, dumbass?"

"She also has a copy."

"Well, that just expanded my search beyond the regular fences." He laughs at his statement. "As they say, 'Love is blind.' Okay, Sal, I have just one more question for you, and this is an important one. Who else knows about your engagement to this broad, and who might want to get back at you for some reason bad enough that they'd kidnap her?"

"Everyone knows I'm engaged to her. We sent out wedding invitations. Didn't you get yours?"

"Yeah, but I thought it might be a small, intimate ceremony or something. What else?"

I sigh, "I don't know who might be mad at me. Maybe… uh… okay, there's Davy. I fucked his little sister, and the next day he came screaming at me that she was a virgin. He socked me so hard; I thought he'd busted my jaw. I've never seen anyone so pissed."

Damien roars with laughter. "He tells everyone that. It's his brand of humor. Try again."

"Oh… uh… I don't know. You figure it out. That's what I'm paying you for."

"Sal, you're hopeless."

"Just do your fucking job. You're giving me a headache."

I hear him muttering "pussy" as he hangs up. Some friend. I hope he comes through pretty soon. The wedding is supposed to be in three days. I guess we might have to cancel. How embarrassing. Someone might think she's a runaway bride instead of being kidnapped. Oh man… *I gotta get my woman back*!

WE DO HAVE TO CANCEL. IT'S NOW PAST THE WEDDING DATE, and we've heard nothing. Her trail is cold, and there is no evidence of anyone seeing her, hearing from her, or anything. I can't believe she'd just disappear from her family or from me like this, so I'm definitely thinking it's foul play now. I'm so upset; I can hardly get out of bed in the morning.

ANOTHER WEEK HAS GONE BY, AND I HAVE GONE FROM sadness to unbelievable anger that this would happen. Hank is on my case about our arrangement, saying the creditors are about to seize his apartment and all of its contents, and he needs cash in the worst way. I know if I don't go through with our plan pretty soon, there won't be any pizza delivery business to use for my purposes, but I've been too much of a mental case to figure out anything else. I'm sick of his whining, but we need to do something quick, Anna or no Anna. I gotta keep my reputation up so I don't lose face because I bragged my ass off to my boss about my great idea. He put a lot of trust in me, and if this fails… heaven help me. I'll be in deep shit. I might lose way more than my reputation.

I call Damien and let him know that Anna's mom and dad are about to get booted out of their apartment. "Is there anything else you can think of to find her? This is such a colossal fuck-up."

He sighs and says, "I'll see if going through their place with a fine-toothed comb gets me any information. What they told me was worthless, but who knows what they've missed with their heads so far up their own asses? I'll get on it today."

I feel marginally better when Damien calls me the next morning. He tells me, "I found an old handwritten phonebook with a bunch of her friends' names in it, so now I have some possible contacts to reach out to. Don't you think her parents would have looked for something like that?" He sighs. "Anyways, I dumped the contents of her drawers into a box that I brought home, and I can look through this crap for clues. Most of it looks pretty old, but at least it's more than we had before."

A few days after that, I call Damien for another update. He sounds frustrated when he says, "Most of those phone numbers were so old they don't even exist anymore, and the few people I did talk to either couldn't remember anyone named Anna or had no idea where she worked or anything about her. She didn't keep in contact with her old friends too well, apparently. But I did find one thing that was sort of curious, and I'm going to take a trip south to see if it means anything. I found this little girlie note that had the name Honeybee Hollow on it, and the name was surrounded by a heart like it meant a lot to her. It sounded familiar, so I looked it up. It's where the former governor of Kentucky grew up, and the town basically became a mecca for tourists because it's so quaint. It might be a worthless longshot, or... who knows? I need a little vacation, so I'm heading down there tomorrow. Beyond this, I've got nothing."

"Well, good luck. But I think it sounds like a dumb idea, so don't go looking at me to pay extra for your expenses."

Eighteen

Blake

I'm in the Hollow Five and Dime on the edge of town discussing a rash of petty thefts—probably kids since most of what's missing is candy—when I get a call from Betty at the Honeybee Hollow Inn. Seeing her number pop up, a chill runs down my back.

"Hey, Betty, what's up?" I try to sound calm.

"Sheriff!" She sounds like she's trying to whisper, but she's too excited. "Something bad is happening… well, maybe. I mean it could be something, if you know what I mean. I'm hiding out in my office right now 'cause I didn't want to call you from the reception desk, but there's this huge guy—really handsome—but he looks like he might be mean and maybe kinda shifty. He just checked in for the night, or maybe he'll stay longer, he said. And then he got all smiley and charming and showed me a photo and asked about someone named Anna. I told him I'd never seen her, but Blake, she looked like she could be your girl Sloane's younger sister. I thought you'd want to know." She finally pauses to take a breath. "I did what you said and told him I didn't know her, and it's not even a lie because I really don't, but…"

"Thanks, Betty," I interrupt her. "You did just fine. Could you do something else for me now and let all your employees and friends know to do exactly what you did? It doesn't matter what he says, no one knows that girl, and they've never seen her. Do *not* mention Sloane, whatever you do. Okay? I gotta run now, but thanks a million. Just stay away from that guy as much as possible, and don't let him see or hear you warning anyone else."

"Yes, yes, I c—"

I hang up before she can keep talking. I need to get to Sloane.

I look at Greg, the store owner, and tell him, "Sorry, I have an emergency. I'll be back later to talk about possible suspects. Just keep your eyes open in the meantime. And if a big guy comes in with a photo of a young woman and he asks about someone named Anna, please be sure to tell him you've never seen or heard of her. This is really important. Tell your employees to do the same. He's possibly dangerous, so interact with him as little as you can."

I hop into my squad car and point it toward Hot Stuff, dialing Juni's number. Fortunately, she answers immediately. "Juni. Emergency. Send Sloane upstairs right now and tell her to lock the deadbolt. Some guy is looking for her and might start asking around town. She's never worked for you, got it? I'll be there in about two minutes. Get Sloane out of there *now*." I don't wait for her answer either and hang up.

Next, I call Sloane, who seems to be running up the stairs as she answers, "What's happening?"

"Someone is looking for you. It doesn't sound like Sal though. Pack your stuff, and I'll be right there to take you to my house. We'll deal with your car later. Do it fast, sweetheart. Don't answer the door for anyone but me. Put on long pants, a hoodie, and sunglasses or a hat if you have one. I'm putting you in the cruiser."

I get stuck behind a school bus because naturally that would happen. And there is a delivery truck blocking the alley behind Hot Stuff, so I'm forced to drive around to park in front of the building. I walk into the coffeehouse to take the shortcut to the back door and see that Brooke has tied a Hot Stuff apron over her baby bump, and she's cheerfully managing the counter sales while Juni arranges a big batch of fresh pastries on a tray. Skyler is busing tables, and Levi is brewing coffees for people. The place is unusually busy, so I feel bad that I had to drag Sloane away from helping Juni. At least Juni has some loyal friends who were ready to help out in a pinch. You gotta love these folks.

I scan the area for any strangers and, seeing only folks I know, I say loudly over the chatter, "Hey, everybody." I have their attention, so I continue, "There's a large man showing a photo around town and asking about a woman named Anna. Steer clear of him. And don't speculate. You don't know anyone named Anna, you've never seen the girl in the photo, and if he persists, you don't know of anyone new in town. That's all you have to tell him. He's possibly dangerous, so I repeat, do not try to engage him in conversation. Please tell your friends to do the same if he confronts them. Thank you for doing your civic duty."

I turn and head out the back and up the stairs. Looking both ways, I see that the delivery truck is still blocking the alley, so Sloane couldn't get her car out now if she wanted to. I ought to ticket the driver just for being an asshole and a nuisance, but I don't have the time. I knock softly on her door and say, "It's me."

She opens the door a crack. I can see the worry on her face for an instant before she closes it to take the chain off. She lets me in, and I can't help but grab her into a tight embrace. She's shaking. She's been able to make quick work of packing since a lot of her stuff is already at my house, and she doesn't have that much anyway.

"We'll put this stuff in the trunk of your car, and I'll have one of the deputies come and get it and drive it over later. I don't want to drag a suitcase out on Main Street in the middle of the day and show everyone you're getting out of here. We don't know who's out there watching in case they've figured out you're working again as a barista."

"I feel terrible leaving Juni in the middle of a rush."

I smile and tell her, "She's completely covered. Brooke, Skyler, and Levi are all filling in. Apparently, it takes all three of them to do your job, so I'm impressed. Now, let's get going." She puts on a large pair of sunglasses and pulls a hood up over her head, covering a lot of her face with it.

The delivery truck is still in the way, so after depositing her stuff in her trunk, we enter the back door of Shoo Buzz—the shoe store next to Hot Stuff. I give the owners there the same spiel about a big guy asking around town about Anna. They seem eager to help by sending a mass text message to all the local merchants to deliver my directive. I thank them sincerely since that's an efficient way to get the word out quickly, then I tell Sloane, "It's showtime. Just in case anyone unsavory is watching, I want you to embrace your inner Meryl Streep and try to act guilty without saying anything." I shock the living daylights out of her, I'm sure, because she gasps when I snap handcuffs on her wrists behind her back. Immediately, her body language shifts. She shuffles out to the sidewalk with her shoulders drooped, looking at the ground, and I shove her carefully into the back of the car like I'm arresting her. She slumps way down in the seat, and off we go.

Once we're out of the main shopping district, Sloane gets the giggles. "I finally got to be handcuffed," she guffaws. "I wish it were more fun though. This is uncomfortable."

"We'll be home in five, and I'll take them off then." I'm having a harder time finding the humor when the Mafia might be in town looking for the woman I love.

I check the mirrors repeatedly to see if anyone seems to be following us. So far, so good.

As soon as we pull up to my house and I let Sloane out of the back of the squad car, I start to unlock the cuffs, but she steps away and looks at me with her head cocked. "Please just remove my sunglasses and hood, Sheriff," she says in a sultry voice. I guess she's still in character, but she's no longer a hoodlum. Now she's a vixen. "Let's go inside and play cocks and rubbers," she says with a wink and then lets out a snort at her goofy play on words.

"You're sure?" My pants are suddenly too tight in a certain area, but that's no excuse for my voice to crack.

She gives me a grin and licks her lips. "Come on, Blake. I've been naughty. Just look at me all handcuffed here. I'm a bad, bad robber, and you're the strict cop."

It's silly, I know, but I can't resist. I rush her into the house and down the hall to the bedroom where I take off her shoes and pants. She looks so strange in a hoodie and cuffs but naked from the waist down. My mouth waters thinking about her juicy pink bits, and I'm throbbing.

I spin her around and ask gruffly, "Do you need to be punished for your misbehavior?" I can't help staring at her perky butt. It's round and perfect, just waiting for me to spank it if that's what she wants.

Sloane's answer is a groan. "Yesss. I've been so bad. I need you to discipline me, Sheriff."

I lay my hand on her buttock and stroke her velvet skin for a long moment. She starts shifting her weight from one leg to the other like she's nervous, so I play a little longer and make her wait for it. I caress her, and just as she's starting to relax, I reach around her and grab her pussy with my other hand, forcing my middle finger inside of her and lay a loud, cracking swat on her ass. Her sharp intake of breath makes my blood boil, but she breathes out, "Thank you. That's better." She takes a few deep breaths and asks, "More, please?" Her pussy is soaked.

"Just a moment. I need to get ready." I lean her over the bed with her ass proudly displaying my reddened handprint. Quickly, I unzip my uniform pants and free my engorged dick. It's positively weeping for some attention, so I reach over and grab a condom out of the bedside table, thinking that we need to have a talk soon about getting rid of rubbers. But this probably isn't the time.

Sloane is lying halfway on the bed, feet on the floor and head turned to look at me when she says, "I've been tested. Can we get rid of those things? I'd love to feel you bare, hot stuff."

I can't believe my ears, so I almost stutter, "Uh, yeah, I've been tested, and I'm negative, I mean the results were negative. I'm actually quite positive about this idea. Uh… ass or pussy? Your choice."

"A little more spanking because I feel extra naughty today, and then pussy, please."

I know she's on the pill because she had to go see someone recently about getting a new prescription, so I toss the condom back into the drawer and position myself behind her again. "Tell me how you've been so naughty and why you need a spanking, Sloane."

"I was a troublemaker and led the Mafia to this sweet little town," she says with a hitch in her voice.

Suddenly this isn't so funny anymore. It's real.

"It wasn't your fault, sweet cheeks, but you do need to learn a lesson." Smack! I swat her other buttock and watch the handprint appear. I'm not spanking her hard at all, but it does make a satisfying noise, and her pale skin reacts beautifully. I drop to my knees, spread her feet apart and kiss her flaming cheeks. I reach around and find her clit with my fingers. Soon I have her gasping and begging for my dick.

"Now, Blake, I *need* you. I feel so empty. Put that monster inside of me and fill me up. *Please.*"

I love it when she begs for me, so I stand back up and swiftly impale her with my shaft. Ye gods! I've never felt such ambrosia in my life; I'm unprotected inside of her. She squeezes me like she wants to strangle a snake. She's so tight, it's almost painful, and the friction as I push in and pull out of her is beyond description. I just know my dick wants to live inside this woman forever. And my heart does as well. It's like my entire being is swallowed up inside of her, and if she ever lets go of me, I'll drop dead. My thoughts are a jumble of mixed metaphors and crazy desire. I just know this woman owns me in a profound way.

In and out I pound and release, stroking and stroking her clit until she hollers, "Yes, yes, yes! That's it, Blake. Don't stop, oh please don't stop." She's shaking and writhing beneath me. It's amazing; I'm experiencing pleasure overload like I've never even dreamed of.

"I'm not stopping, sweet love. Come for me as much as you can. Let it all go." I end on a groan as I erupt inside her with a massive load of cum, jerking and shaking until I'm all wrung out. She's panting heavily, but her spasms have stopped. I realize she might be getting pretty uncomfortable in this position, so I slide out and step back. I help her to her feet and stare like a greedy fool as my load begins to drip down her thighs. "Gorgeous," I whisper. "Perfect."

Sloane laughs softly and adds, "Messy, but sexy. Okay, you can uncuff me now so I can clean up." She winks at me and adds, "That was fun, and I love it that you didn't even get undressed. That made it extra naughty."

"I didn't want to waste the time," I confess.

"Exactly. I do love an eager man."

"Good." The words "I love you too" just kind of fly out of my mouth before my brain catches up to what I just said—and what she may or may not have actually meant by her statement.

She blinks for an instant and then smiles. "Well then, if

you love me as much as I love you, we'd better kiss and make it official."

"I've never been this happy, Sloane. Not ever." I seal her lips with the kind of kiss that starts somewhere around my heart and wraps around my lips.

She returns it in what feels the same way, but finally we break apart and she asks, "Cuffs, please?"

"Oh damn, I'm sorry. Right away." I fish around for the keys for a moment hoping for a couple of scary seconds that I didn't drop them somewhere. "Ah, here you go!" I release her, and she rubs her reddened wrists.

"I think I want to go sit in a bathtub. Can you join me?" she asks.

"Unfortunately, I need to leave because I have some other business to handle. I'm sorry. But I'll bring us home some dinner later, and we can do whatever you like then." She nods, so I go clean up and turn on the tub for her. Soon she joins me in the bathroom without the rest of her clothes. I lend her a hand to help her into the tub. "I left some arnica ointment on the counter for you in case your bottom hurts."

"It's fine, but thank you."

She's so perfect. And she's mine.

CHAPTER
Nineteen

It was hard to leave Sloane, but I'm pretty positive no one knows she's here. I told her that I would turn on the alarm when I left and gave her the alarm code and the fob with the panic button on it. I rarely ever think of using the system, but in this case, I'm glad I installed it last year. She promised not to leave the house, so I'm glad I have hundreds of books she can choose from to keep her occupied. My tastes in literature are eclectic, so she ought to be able to find something. And there's always Netflix.

When I get back to town, I stop in and check with Juni and let her know Sloane is safe. But when I enter Hot Stuff, my heart almost stops as I hear what she's telling a large stranger who's holding a photograph up to her.

"Hmm," she says. "Yeah, I can't be positive, but I'm pretty sure that's the girl I talked to. She came in here a couple of weeks ago asking about a job. But I didn't have any openings, so I sent her up to a restaurant some friends of mine own in Berea. They told me the other day they were looking for a couple of waitresses, and they were swamped with business. So I told her how to get to Berea, and she lit out of here like she couldn't get there fast enough. I haven't seen her since."

"Berea, you say? Is that in Kentucky?" Juni nods. "What's the name of the restaurant?" he asks.

"Oh, it's one of those crunchy places with a name like Joyful Earth or Healthy Planet or something like that. I always forget. But it's painted blue—I think—and has a cute sign out front. I hope you find your sister, sir."

"What street is it on?"

"Oh, yeah… um… it might be the name of a tree… or a flower… or something about bluegrass. I'm sorry, I've only been there once, and it was quite a while back. We just keep in touch mostly through social media."

"Okay, thank you. You've been quite helpful." He brushes past me while I try to look as though I'm studying the menu board behind the counter. But behind my wraparound sunglasses, I'm really studying him. He's just as Betty described—handsome, smooth, and dangerous-looking. He obviously didn't want to make eye contact with me and seemed to pause for a split second when he saw my uniform. This makes me flash back to some of the things Grover taught me about looking for tells in crooks. Grover's lessons have been invaluable over the years. This guy's body language announced that he didn't want to get near me, but it was too late to turn around once he discovered that I was behind him. He compensated by spending a lot of effort looking toward the inside pocket of his jacket where he was returning the photograph. He easily could have slipped it in there without bending his face down to look at it.

I wait a few moments and slip out the door behind him, watching as he makes his way back to the inn. He's walking purposely as if he's on a mission, but he's also typing something—probably directions—into his phone. I trail him at a distance until I see him head into the Honeybee Hollow Inn. Fairly certain I know what will happen next, I wait around for another five minutes, then see him rush out the door again, holding a travel bag. He gets into a car that looks like a rental. I step back into the shadow of a recessed doorway, and as he drives past me in the direction of the highway, I jot down the make and license number of the car.

My phone rings, and it's Betty, who tells me breathlessly, "Sheriff! That icky guy just dropped off his key and lit outta here! I asked him if something was wrong 'cause he was carrying his suitcase. He just said he won't be back. Didn't even ask for a refund for not staying. Seemed to be in an awful big hurry if you ask me."

"Yeah, thanks Betty, I saw him leave. You got a name for him, didn't you? Did he use a credit card?"

"No, he paid cash up front, but he signed the register. Let me look." She takes a moment, and I hear a grumble from her. "Blake, you still there?"

"Yes. What do you know?"

"His handwriting is pretty bad, but I think it says his name is John Hancock. What a shifty no-good who thinks he's funny."

"Just great. Okay, thanks Betty. If he comes back, you'll call me immediately, won't you?"

"You can count on me, Sheriff. Now take good care of that lovely Sloane, alright?"

"Will do. And one of these days I may have to deputize you. Great job."

"Oh, go on, you sweet-talker. Bye-bye."

My temper is starting to boil over by the time I get back to Juni's place, so fortunately the customers have all left and she's only there with Brooke. "What the hell were you thinking, Juni?" I storm at her as soon as I cross the threshold.

She looks at me benignly and says, "I was giving you some time to figure out what to do with Sloane by sending him on a wild goose chase. If we're lucky, he'll never show up again."

"And if he does come back once he realizes you lied to him, you're in danger! He's a terrible person, Juni. That was reckless of you." I glower at her, but she simply stares me down. I'll say one thing for our Juni—she has a backbone of steel. Still, I'm not finished with my tirade. "We also don't know if he's here by himself. There might be others looking for Sloane. We have reason to believe this guy and that jerk Sal she told you about are connected to the Mafia, and *they don't mess around.*"

Juni gives me a cocky grin and says, "As much as I adore Sloane, for a lawman, you sure managed to get wrapped up with an interesting girlfriend. Aren't you worried she could be detrimental to your career?"

A growl burns up from my gut when I grit my teeth and say, "Sloane *has* to stay safe." And then I burst out with, "I... I'm in love with her!"

"Woohoo!" Juni cheers and immediately does a high five with Brooke, who is grinning ear to ear. "Finally! We did it, Brooke!"

"Yes!" Brooke does a little happy dance. "From Grumpy Gus to Loverboy," she chortles and then stage-whispers to Juni, "*Still seems a little grumpy though.*" She looks at me and says, "Maybe you ought to take the rest of the day off, Blake. Go home to cool down. Or maybe heat up... you know? With Sloane." She laughs at her own joke.

I don't understand women. These two ought to be worried for their friend, and yet they act like they won the lottery. I choose to ignore their behavior.

I straighten my already stiff posture and, in my best

taking-evidence voice, I ask, "So who do you know in Berea? Was there any truth to that part of your story?"

"Sure. I sent him to my hippie parents' organic health food restaurant. It looks somewhat the way I described, but the name is Global Goodies. I always thought it was kind of a dumb name, but they have an extremely loyal customer base, even though there is a lot of competition in the organic restaurant market in that city. There are a lot of college kids as well as the kookie artist types living there, and they really go for that stuff. He'll waste a bunch of time trying to find the place, so that'll keep him occupied even longer. My parents run the restaurant themselves, and they're fully staffed. They don't need any waitresses. I was just about to call them and let them know that a big jerk is probably going to show up later today asking about a woman named Anna. You can talk to them too if you want."

"Nice of you," I tell her flatly. "Can you go ahead and alert them now? I might also call the Berea police about him, although he hasn't done anything that's against the law that I know of. Yet."

Juni grins and grabs her phone. After a few seconds, she says cheerfully, "Hi, Daddy! Can you talk a minute? I need to tell you something kind of important. Mama needs to hear it too." She waits while he answers, "Okay. Hi, Mama! I know you're busy, so I'll cut to the chase. It's highly likely that later today—maybe during dinner or possibly tomorrow—there'll be a tall, good-looking man—sort of forties-ish—who's going to come to your place with a photo, and he's going to ask if a woman named Anna works there for you. He's kind of a bad dude, so don't offer more information than is totally necessary, but tell him she applied for the job, and you hired her a couple of weeks ago, but she didn't like it and left after only a few days. You also need to tell him she mentioned going back to New York because she was really unhappy in Kentucky. If he asks to see any paperwork or pretends to be a cop, don't believe him and tell him to get lost. He might also say Anna is his sister, but she isn't. Tell your staff to say the same thing if he questions them." She waits again and listens while someone asks a question, then answers, "Anna is someone who needs to stay hidden, and this guy is *really* bad news. I know you can deal with him though. I'll let you get back to work. I'm just closing up for the day, but we'll talk soon." Pausing, Juni gives me a questioning look, and I shake my head. I have nothing to add. She finishes up with her parents, "Yes, the guys are both fine, and we're anxious for you to come visit us and see the new house. Let me know if the creepy guy shows up, okay? Love you both. Bye." She smirks at me with a proud yet cunning expression.

Nodding, I tell her, "Juni, you have a devious mind. I'm rather impressed, and I hope your wild goose chase leads this creep back up north and out of the state. But we'll have to wait and see."

"Can Sloane come back to work?" she asks hopefully. "It gets pretty crazy around here when it's just me."

I shake my head, and Brooke pipes up, "I can do it."

Juni looks worried as she says, "Oh, no. You're getting too close to your due date. I don't want to wear you out by keeping you on your feet, and your guys would probably have a fit. Today was a one-time thing, and it didn't last all day. Plus, they did most of the heavy lifting."

Brooke sighs. "You're right, I guess. And I haven't exactly taken maternity leave from my regular job yet. The company would probably appreciate it if I finished up my current project before I take off for a couple of months."

I can't help thinking that Brooke is such a loyal friend. "I'm sorry to leave you short-handed, Juni. I'll ask around and see if someone can pitch in for a while."

"I'll ask Skyler's mom too. She knows every last person in this town," Brooke adds. "In fact, I'll call her right now." She whips her phone out of her pocket and says, "Tracy, hi! I have a question for you." They go back and forth for a while and then she hangs up beaming at Juni. "She has a bunch of ideas, so hopefully you'll have help by the morning."

CHAPTER

Twenty

SALVATORE CAPUTO

"ARE YOU *SHITTING* ME?" I RAGE AT DAMIEN. "YOU DROVE all over Ken-fucking-tucky looking for my fiancée, and they said she came back to *New York*? I'm calling those no-good parents of hers immediately. No! On second thought, I'm going over there to see if they're hiding Anna from me." I stomp around grabbing my keys and wallet, muttering, "They'll be sorry, those stupid morons."

"Want me to join you?" Damien asks me calmly. "I can be quite persuasive."

"Uh, yeah, sure. Let's go." I appreciate muscle when it's on my side.

So we hightail it over to their apartment, and Mrs.

Dumbass opens the door looking tired and frazzled. She may even have been crying. I'm not letting some lady tears sway me though. I push the door open and demand, "Where is she?"

"Where's who? What's the matter with you?"

"Anna, you stupid bitch!" I grab her arms for emphasis as I get right up in her face. I want her to *feel* my anger.

Her eyes go huge, and she gasps just as her husband shows up, bellowing, "Get your hands off my wife! What's the matter with you?"

"Anna's here, isn't she? She's not in Kentucky. They said she came back here."

"Kentucky? What? Who?" He looks more perplexed than I expected. I was sure he'd look guilty.

"The hippies," I blurt out and realize immediately that my answer sounds ridiculous, but it is what it is.

"Wha…? Look, Sal, let's all go sit down. We'll have a glass of wine and discuss this. We haven't seen Anna, so I don't know what you're carrying on about."

Damien and I follow him into his office while his wife goes off to scare up a bottle of red. My heartbeat is still pounding in my ears, I'm so angry. I gotta calm the fuck down. He sits behind his desk like he's all important and shit, and we take the two chairs across from him, even though I find it hard to sit still. He glares at me a second and then asks, "Care to explain why you barged in here and scared my wife half to death?"

I look at Damien, and he begins to tell his story about

trailing Anna to Honeybee Hollow in Kentucky. Her dad claims to have never heard of the place, which I find odd. How would she know about the place then? Didn't Damien say it looked like it was written by a kid? Well, maybe she heard about it at school.

Damien continues in a clipped voice, "It's a small town— very attractive, and the vibe there is friendly and upbeat. I showed Anna's photo around to a few people who claimed to have never seen her, but then I saw a coffeehouse and thought to myself she might have gotten a job there as a barista again." Her dad sits forward and perks up at this. "But when I talked to the proprietor, she told me she *had* seen Anna but wasn't interested in hiring her because she was fully staffed. There were at least three other people working in the place, so that seemed legit. Then she told me she sent Anna to some friends of hers in another larger city called Berea because they needed a couple of waitresses for their restaurant. It sounded like Anna was interested, so I thought I'd follow the trail. She sent me up there with the barest description of the building, and she wasn't sure of the name, so it took me a while to locate the place she meant.

"It turned out to be an organic health-food restaurant run by an older pair of hippies who serve the worst meals in the world. I ordered a burger, hoping if I stuck around a while I'd see Anna. The so-called burger turned out to be all smooshed up vegetables and mushrooms, and it gave me the worst case of gas ever. Burger, my ass. A guy like me needs his meat." He shudders. "Anna was nowhere to be seen. Anyway, I finally got to talk to the owners, and they told me they had hired Anna, and she worked there for a while, but she was unhappy and went back to New York. Since she doesn't have an apartment anymore, we figured she'd show back up here." Damien stands and leans over the desk with his hands resting on the surface and scowls in Mr. Dumbass's face. "You must have *heard* from her at least. So what information are you holding out on and why?" His voice could cut through granite.

Daddy Dearest's face goes pale. He shifts his eyes to me, and his voice shakes as he answers, "Sal, you gotta believe me. Anna isn't here, and we haven't heard a word from her. Maybe she went to stay with a friend."

"What friend?" I ask, skewering him with the Caputo Eye. "Gimme a name."

"Uh…" he stalls. "Maybe we should call the police and report a missing person."

"Right. You do that. Because we really need the cops sniffing around. In the meantime, Damien here is going to go check her bedroom to see if she's *in it*."

Damien nods and marches through the door just as the wife arrives with three burgundy-hued drinks on a tray. She shrieks like a banshee as the wineglasses go flying. The glasses shatter, and there's red wine everywhere—but mostly all over her. This meeting is going to hell.

Damien barely pauses though and stomps away down the hall. I swear, the smell of that wine is so strong and awful, it must be called Rotgut Red. It sure isn't anything I'd ever want to drink. Damien's collision with the tray was a mercy killing.

A moment later, Damien stalks back into the room, stepping over the mess, and he announces, "The room's empty and it doesn't look like anyone's been living in it since the last time I checked it out."

"Just great. So now how do we find her?" I ask, flinging my hands in the air.

"You could ask around at her college and see if anyone remembers who she hung out with," her dad offers.

I roll my eyes and give him a look. "It's been a few years since she graduated, Einstein. Her friends are all gone by now, and you think her professors would even remember her? They see hundreds of kids a year, and I'm sure they don't pay any attention to who hangs out with who. Try again."

Damien clears his throat. "I think the hippies were lying to me," he says with narrowed eyes. "There was something fishy about their story."

"What?"

"It all felt too rehearsed. They seemed to have a script to stick to, and the words they used didn't fit their personalities. When they were done telling me she'd lit out for New York, they couldn't get away from me fast enough. I shoulda asked some of the employees if they'd ever seen Anna working there and not just the owners." He sighs. "I can't believe I fell for it. Those sneaky hippies lied to me—I'm sure of it now!" He looks at me with resolve. "Probably all of those fuckwads in Honeybee Hollow were lying through their teeth too."

"What's this about Honeybee Hollow?" Mrs. Dumbass asks as she reenters the room with new glasses of wine. She looks like she just stabbed someone with those red stains all over her dress.

Damien answers, "I found a note in her drawer saying Honeybee Hollow on it and thought it might be a clue. You know anything?"

"She did mention it once or twice when she was little. I thought she'd read about it in one of her storybooks or made it up. It's a real place?"

Ignoring her question, Damien says with a frown, "I need to get back to Kentucky,"

"You sure you don't just have some broad you fell for down there you wanna bang? And you wanna do it on my dime?" I ask. "I told you I wasn't paying any more expenses for your vacations."

He snorts. "Believe me, the women in that town are spec-tacular, but I was on a mission. No banging. Well… unless one of 'em asks me real nice." He gives me another one of his looks and asks, "Ya wanna come with me this time? I really think Anna is still there, and maybe only you can persuade her to come back."

"Well… I don't like to fly." I squirm in my seat a little because admitting that makes me feel like a wuss.

"Fine, I'll drive us. I hated that rental car I got in

Lexington anyway. Piece a shit, and it smelled like cheap perfume."

"Alright. I'll go." I glare at Daddy Dumbass. "I'll find Anna myself. And if I find you've been lying to us and you did know where Anna was all this time, we'll fit you for some nice custom cement shoes, and you're gonna be the sorriest hunk of fish bait on the bottom of the Atlantic."

He was pale before, but now he looks like he's about to barf. His wife gasps, and he chokes out, "I swear, Sal. I don't know where that crazy kid is. You have to believe me. We're going to be partners soon, I promise. It'll be great—just like you said."

I wish I had a nickel for every time I heard someone swear to me they were telling the truth. I'd be a... well... an even richer man than I already am.

Unfortunately, because of some "business dealings" I have scheduled for the next two days, we can't leave right away. There are just some things I can't trust to any of my guys. I delegate what I can, but the heavy stuff, I handle. I'd look weak if I didn't do it myself.

But now, New York is less one double-crossing informant and an undercover cop who wouldn't play nice, my deliveries are all up to date with explicit instructions for handling more, and I'm finally ready to head out of town with Damien. He tried again—unsuccessfully—to get me to fly down there, citing all kinds of statistics, but I held my ground. Literally. I held onto the fucking ground like I'm permanently affixed to it, and I like it that way. I don't even like high-rise buildings. Flying is for birds, bats, and bugs. And I'm not too crazy about them either.

CHAPTER
Twenty~One

Sloane

Staying at Blake's house is great. I never knew how tightly wound I was until I found myself in this perfectly quiet place with nothing I needed to accomplish for a few weeks. Sure, I've done a little laundry, housekeeping, and fixed food when I needed it, but I've had all the time in the world to stare out the window and enjoy the sight of the surrounding forest where I've watched birds, squirrels, raccoons, foxes, and plenty of deer go about their business. I've read some really great books and filled a notebook with ideas for teaching acting classes and creating a local playhouse. Blake checks in with me several times a day, so I haven't gotten lonely, and Juni stops by after she closes Hot Stuff for the afternoon.

Sometimes Brooke comes with her when she isn't busy. She's getting big!

And speaking of Brooke, she mentioned recently that the Colfax family has three lovely female Labradors. It made me think about how much Blake would love to get a dog, so I promised myself to look into it. He also has a birthday coming up, and I think that would be an amazing gift for him.

It turns out that Tracy Colfax, Skyler's mom, rounded up several friends who came in to help Juni in pairs. They refused to take a dime, so Juni sent them all home with pastries. I love the people in this town, but I also wonder how long we can sustain this. Tracy's friends will need to get back to their regular lives, and I need to get out of the house at some point. It's been quite a while now, and no one has seen or heard anything strange about mafiosos invading Kentucky looking for a runaway bride. I think it's time to discuss my "release from captivity" with Blake.

It's not that I mind being sequestered here. I feel safe and protected, and having Blake to myself is... well, it's an unending fantasy. That man is sex on wheels. He's attentive and loving. He makes me feel like the most important woman in the world to him—so I guess I am. And making love to him is transcendental. When he's feeling aggressive, he's like an animal. He's big and strong and surrounds me with his passion. He nips and pinches and fucks harder than a jackhammer when he's in that kind of mood. God, I love it, and I can't get enough.

He can also be a gentle lover. He's always been somewhat unpredictable with his temperament, but now he channels that into the different ways we have sex. He sometimes strokes and kisses me from top to bottom, relishing every inch of me until I'm begging him to slam that big dick into me and *fuck*. But he'll chuckle and slow down, torturing me with beautiful affection. It won't change until I'm drowning in need, and only then will he slide into me and slowly bring me to astounding ecstasy.

When he's feeling playful or bossy—those moods seem closely related—he'll spank me. I can't even believe how much I crave that. Maybe some psychologist would have a field day with my need to be spanked after growing up largely ignored and craving attention, but I don't care. I just know it makes me get so hot I feel like steam is pouring off of me. Sometimes, after giving me a good spanking, he'll carefully make love to my butt, and once in a while he'll use a dildo in my pussy at the same time. Wow. I never thought I'd like either of those activities, but I'm starting to crave anal. It makes me feel like I've been punished for my transgressions, then I've gotten a reprieve, but then I'm naughty all over again. It's a mind fuck.

No matter what we do or how we do it in bed, his words are always full of love. He's still trying out silly pet names for me, and some are way better than others, but he always lets me know that he loves me. So even if I'd like to get out of the house and lead a normal life not worrying that some Mafia asshole is looking for me, I'm satisfied that I have the best man in the world right here in Honeybee Hollow.

Blake called me about an hour ago to say he'd be home as soon as he finished some paperwork and would pick up dinner for us from the restaurant at the Honeybee Hollow Inn. Their food is always fantastic, no matter what they fix, so I'm looking forward to whatever he brings. It's time for me to spruce up a little because he ought to be home any minute.

As soon as I've brushed my hair and brushed my teeth, I hear Blake entering through the kitchen door, so I rush out to greet him. It turns out dinner is an Asian-inspired chicken and vegetable stir fry that smells so good, I can't wait to try it. "This is one of my favorites," he tells me and proceeds to pull a mountain of food out of the bags he brought in.

"So, Blake…" I begin, and he looks at me questioningly while we enjoy our meal. I can see why he likes it so much. "I've been making some calls, and I have a bit of a surprise for your birthday tomorrow."

"Oh?"

"Yes, but it's something that's actually so personal, I'm not sure I ought to handle it on my own. You need to have a say. If you want to weigh in, it will ruin the surprise, but you need to be perfectly comfortable with the decision for it to be a success. If you don't like the idea, I'll just bake you a cake instead."

He frowns lightly and asks, "Um… what are you talking about?"

"Well," I take a deep breath and then let my words tumble out. "I've found you a dog. He sounds perfect, and he needs a home. He's five months old, very friendly, and housebroken, but the breeder had to take him back last week when the family who originally took him discovered their little boy was terribly allergic, and with his asthma it turned out to be a large problem for them. They're heartbroken, but the fact is the pup is back at the breeder's place, and she needs to rehome him."

Blake's eyes look glassy as he asks, "What kind of dog is he?"

"Oh, sorry. I should have mentioned he's a black Labrador, and the breeder is about half an hour away."

"Can we go get him tomorrow?" he asks with an enormous grin. "It's my day off."

"Sure, we can. I'm as anxious to meet him as you are. She says he has a wonderful personality. She would keep him herself, but she already has too many dogs."

"This is going to be the best birthday I've ever—no *anyone's* ever had. I can't thank you enough, puppy love."

I snicker at the dumb name and say, "Well, you haven't met him yet, so let's go see him. I'll call right now and set up a time that's good for the breeder."

Blake gets out of his chair, kneels beside me, and wraps his strong arms around me, burying his face in my hair. "I love you so much, Sloane," he whispers.

THE PUPPY IS PERFECT. THE MOMENT HE SEES BLAKE, HE wags his tail hard and fast, throwing his whole body into it. Pretty soon, his butt might fall off if he keeps that up. Blake drops to the floor to sit beside him, draws the pup into his arms, and holds him with happy tears falling into his shiny coat. I've never seen anything like it. They kiss and hug each other, and you'd swear they'd been best friends in a previous life the way they get along. My eyes get watery just watching them, and the breeder looks on with a delighted expression. This dog has the sweetest face I've ever seen. He's just gorgeous, and judging from the size of his paws, he still has a lot of growing to do.

Blake looks up at the breeder and asks, "What's his name?"

"Oh, that's for you to decide. Just start calling him whatever you want, and he'll catch on right away," she answers with a smile.

Blake looks at the puppy, and with a crack in his voice, he says, "Hi there, Grover."

"Oh, Blake," I say as a tear streaks down my face. "That's the perfect way to honor your old friend."

"Some things have a wonderful way of working out, don't they?" the breeder asks. "The previous owners called to say they'd found a Portuguese water dog that's hypoallergenic for their little boy yesterday, so now everyone is happy."

We go over vet visits, vaccinations, diet, training, and all sorts of things with the breeder. She gives us a folder with lots of great information about taking care of a puppy as well as Grover's bloodline and the history of Labradors. She suggests some foods she likes to feed her dogs, and Blake assures her he knows a terrific vet practice in Honeybee Hollow. Then we discover that Tracy and Mike Colfax have gotten a few of their Labs from this same breeder over the years. Small world. She gives us a packet of food that's enough for a few days, I write her a check, and finally we're on our way.

Our first stop is the local pet shop where we get a large crate, a dog bed, a ton of toys—including a squeaky blue Grover toy because we couldn't resist—some more food, shampoo, and a sturdy leash. We also discover that while there aren't any group dog training classes in our area, there is a well-respected trainer who can come to the house and work with us. Everything is looking terrific.

While Blake is busy securing Grover into his new car harness, I send a quick text to Juni so she can set the rest of the day's plans in motion.

When we get back to his house, Blake is dumbfounded to see his driveway filled with cars, and when we step out, the aroma of barbecue fills the air. "What did you do?" he asks me with a huge grin. I love to see this man with a happy smile.

"Let's get Grover on his leash and take him out back where he can meet everyone," I tell him with a wink.

So we round the house, and all of our friends turn to Blake and cry, "Surprise! Happy birthday!" Someone shoves a beer into his hand, and several people ooh and ahh over Grover. The pup seems to be dealing with the crowd of new people like a champ. He shakes hands and kisses anybody who gets close enough to him. At least he's not a shy dog. In fact, he adores the attention.

Asher is manning the grill, and when Blake asks if he needs any help, Asher tells him, "Sit down and enjoy the day. We all know how hard you work to keep our town safe, so this is the day for us to take care of you."

Juni leads Blake to a lawn chair and makes a big fuss over Grover. She's smitten. I know she wants a dog too. She turns to me and whispers, "It's like you two have started your family already with the puppy." I can't help grinning at the thought.

The birthday party is a huge success. Juni brought an enormous chocolate cake she'd baked, and everyone else brought drinks, the fixings for burgers, salads, casseroles, and all sorts of favorites. Several people take turns playing fetch with Grover until he's happily exhausted. I set his dog bed next to Blake, and Grover curls up in it finally and goes to sleep. Blake can't stop reaching down to stroke the sleeping pup's coat.

After we all sing "Happy Birthday" and pig out on cake,

Levi gets out his guitar and launches into a string of original songs and favorite ballads. As the sun goes down, it paints the sky an exquisite rose color, and I think I could sit here listening to Levi's music forever. Looking at Blake and Grover together, I feel utter contentment for maybe the first time ever.

We say goodbye finally to our last guests, and Blake turns to me. "This was without a doubt the best day of my life." I know what he means. "But I also know things will heat up later, and we can have even more fun." He gives my bottom a playful squeeze.

Yes, indeed we will. I have plans for this man.

OVER THE NEXT SEVERAL DAYS, WE ESTABLISH A SCHEDULE that suits us with Grover, and he settles in like he owns the place. I find that he's great company when Blake has to be off at work, and while I know the dog loves me, it's Blake he's devoted to. Each time Blake walks into the room, Grover treats him like a returning hero. Exuberance abounds with this pup, and that has to be good for Blake's ego.

One of the games we inadvertently invented that Grover seems to love is hide-and-seek. One of us will hide, and the other will command Grover to "find Blake" or "find Sloane," and he'll go zooming off. He's wonderful at it and always looks so proud when he's found the person who's hiding.

I especially enjoy exploring the woods that surround the house with Grover. We're planning to put an invisible perimeter fence in to keep him contained safely when he's out by himself but that won't disturb the wildlife. The installers should be here in a couple of days. Grover loves watching the squirrels, and he's sniffed every inch of Blake's land, probably relishing the smells of the local fauna. Blake insists, however, that each time I'm outdoors, I have to have the panic button on me at all times. He still is not convinced that the coast is clear from Sal and his goons, so he put the fob on a leather cord that I wear around my neck.

That's about the only thing marring our otherwise idyllic life, and I try to forget about the threat as much as I can.

But then… I can no longer ignore it.

Oh, God. No!

CHAPTER

Twenty-Two

Salvatore Caputo

On our way down to Bumfuckytucky, Damien and I discuss the way we want to approach finding Anna *this* time. I'm still pretty pissed at Damien for falling for the story of a couple of dumbass hippies. He should have used his damn head.

It's a long-as-fuck drive—like twelve hours or something, so we have plenty of time for strategizing. I brought my fake police ID, so that's the way we'll approach it to start out.

I get antsy sitting in a car too long, so we end up spending the night twice on the way down there—first in Pittsburgh and the second night in Cincinnati. I guess there is a shorter route, but our maps app directed us along this route to avoid road construction.

Anyways, I get leg cramps from sitting still too long, so we stop when I say so, and that generally coincides with when I'm good and ready for a drink.

First thing we do in Berea is find accommodations in a decent hotel and then head over to Global Goodies. For fuck's sake, who names a restaurant that? Maybe it resonates with the tie-dye and patchouli crowd, but I think it sounds ridiculous. We park down the street on accounta Damien was already here kinda recently, and we don't want him freaking out anyone who saw him asking around already.

It's just about time for the dinner rush when I walk over and hang around near the entrance, but not too close so's I'm disturbing the hippies, or rather tipping them off that I'm asking questions. I conjure up my most sincere smile and stop a couple who are heading toward the place, flash my badge quickly, and laugh to myself when they flinch. I know the marijuana laws in this state aren't as liberal as New York. Like I give a shit if they light up on the regular.

"'Scuse me, I'm lookin' for a missing person and have reason to believe this restaurant was the last place around here she was seen," I say trying to sound like a cop. I pull out Anna's photo, ready to give them a good long look. "I'm trying to verify that information. Do you eat here often?"

"Usually about once a week or so," the man answers me. "The way they fix lentils is fantastic. I strongly recommend them if you can stop in for supper. Lots of flavor, so... uh... yeah. Great protein source..."

I've heard enough about their stupid lentils, so I interrupt, "This young lady is named Anna Sloane, and we understand she worked here. Is she familiar to you?" I hold the photo up to them.

They both look baffled and shake their heads. The wife answers, "She's never worked here that I know of, and we're friends with the owners."

"I see. Well, you've been most helpful. Please enjoy your meal, and I won't bother you anymore."

They look back over their shoulders at me again before opening the front door and disappearing inside. They seemed honest enough to me. But to be on the safe side, I stop a few more people headed toward the place. One group is a bunch of college kids who have never been here before but were looking for a good vegetarian place to have dinner. They're no help. So I keep it up with more folks, and each time I get the same response—they eat here frequently, and they've never seen Anna. One guy starts to add something about the wait-staff being employed there a long time, but the woman with him contradicts him and says, "Now we don't know that for sure. Maybe this Anna woman worked here, and we missed her."

Still, this all adds up to the owners giving Damien a phony baloney load of crap when he questioned them. Maybe it was on accounta the case of gas he had, and they didn't want him sticking around. But I think they were lying through their teeth to him. I head back to the car and yank the door open. Damien's playing some game on his phone and jumps about a foot when I flop inside.

"I need a drink," I announce. "Those jerks lied their asses off to you. We need to head over to Honeybee Hollow in the morning, but right now I'd like a bottle of whiskey and a willing broad so's I can blow off some steam. Let's go."

Before we can find a bar that will fulfill my needs, I decide to recruit more muscle. I make a couple of phone calls to New York, and I'm satisfied we'll have some backup after the guys land in Lexington in the morning and rent a car. There's no big rush yet because we still need to figure out where Anna is hiding. I do know who must have a pretty good idea though— that bitch with the coffee place. She started all that rigmarole by sending Damien on a wild goose chase. We'll have to deal with her.

Nobody crosses Sal Caputo.

After driving around Berea, we finally decide that if I'm gonna get laid, I'll have to use a dating app. This place is too wholesome for the kind of fun I need. But when I fail miserably at that as well, I'm in a shitty mood. We go back to the hotel, order dinner, and polish off some decent local bourbon.

My mood is even shittier when I wake up with a raging headache. I'm so pissed off I decide the whole thing is Anna's fault. How could I ever have thought I might actually love her? This woman has caused me all kinda grief. Oh, who am I kidding? I'm so in love with her I'm obsessed about finding her. And I *know* she's crazy about me! You can't fake that kind of devotion. If I can't find her and rescue her, I won't have the heart to go into business with her dumbass father, and I'll have to figure out another way to get my product delivered around the city in an efficient and sneaky way. Her father is so stupid, I have the man wrapped around my little finger, so he was the best possible partner. He's nothing but a scared chump who's used to a lifestyle he can no longer afford, and his wife is a useless airhead who can barely boil water. Swear to God— they were perfect. Of course, I had a pretty strong hand in causing his business to collapse in the first place by paying his drivers to fuck up on purpose and tampering with the trucks so the food they delivered was stone cold. People don't like that, so vendors stopped using his service. They lost out to Door-Dash in a big, fat hurry, even though it costs more to use them.

Once I get Anna back, if I find out she *wasn't* kidnapped, I sure do want to teach her a lesson. But that's crazy thinking. I'll enjoy getting revenge on her kidnappers, that's for sure. She'll thank me. She's nuts about me.

AFTER ABOUT A GALLON OF COFFEE AND A BIG, GREASY breakfast, my headache's gone, but I'm getting antsy again. Luckily for Damien, the other guys show up just when I'm about to take his head off for failing to find Anna the first time he was down here. We take our meeting up to my room and come up with another plan.

Part discovery and part vengeance. I like the sound of that.

One thing is for sure though, we're not announcing our arrival by booking that local hotel this time. "That innkeeper seemed a little too friendly for my taste," Damien tells us. "And she'll probably recognize me, so I don't want to show up with three other guys this time looking like an army. If we don't find Anna right away, we can go to some other town nearby, and if we do, we'll have to leave Honeybee Hollow immediately anyways."

"Glad to see you're using your head," I tell him. "This time." I'm feeling a little less pissed off at him, but he's going to have to do a lot more to get back in my good graces after that long trip down here. I have important things to do in New York.

On the drive over to Honeybee Hollow, I can't believe the scenery. It's all green and hilly with road signs around every bend advertising campgrounds and lakes, boat rentals, fishing, and all kind of outdoorsy shit like that. Who can honestly stand to live like this? It kinda gives me the creeps—like maybe some backwoods cousin fuckers are going to start shooting at each other and we'll get caught in the crossfire. Where are the buildings? I *need* the sights and smells of Manhattan. Here everything is all about Daniel Boone and Cumberland Falls. Southern barbecue? What's that? Give me some New York cheesecake, street vendor hot dogs, and of course New York pizza. And if I want nature, I'll just look out my window at Central Park. Hiking? No way. The only thing I can see that redeems this area at all is that there are bourbon distilleries all over the place. Now we're talking; that's a tradition I can get behind. If I weren't in a hurry to get home, I might look into the Bourbon Trail tours I keep seeing ads for. What a pity I'll have to miss it.

After this lesson in Kentucky culture from the safe confines of the car, I'm sure Anna will be happy for me to rescue her and take her back to civilization. She hasta be going stir-crazy if she's still here. I can't imagine why she'd choose a place like this. She musta been kidnapped and brought down here. Well… then I remember I'm mad as hell at her for deserting me before the wedding. I need some fucking answers. Did she disappear on her own, or was she kidnapped? All I know is one minute she's hot for me, and the next she's gone. One minute I'm furious with her thinking she left me, and the next I'm positive someone nabbed her. I'm going fucking crazy, and it's all her fault. Fuck… love is hard.

Maybe I'll just march into the police station when we get there, flash my fake badge real quick, and report a possible kidnapping that has led me to their town. I can claim I'm a detective working on the case. Hmm. I like this idea. Might save me a lot of time.

About half an hour later, we're driving through the Honeybee Hollow downtown district, which is so quaint it gives me a toothache. It's too sunny, too colorful, and people are making eye contact and smiling at each other for some reason. Must be something wrong with 'em. I haven't seen a taxi anywhere, and no one's honking. It's just not right.

What I do see are flowers in the windows of boutiques, parents with happy kids eating ice cream cones. The whole place looks like a movie set. Then I spot the sheriff station up ahead and tell Damien, "Pull over. I have some business I want to handle. Park here and stay in the car." I can't believe there are empty parking places right where you need 'em. The other guys pull in next to us as I climb out and stretch.

Gah. It smells like trees and flowers in this place. Where are the real city smells of piss and exhaust? Seriously, how do people stand this much fresh air? And it's so quiet, it makes me jumpy.

"Stay put," I order the other guys. "I'll be back in a minute." I pat my pocket to make sure my "ID" is in place.

The office is a couple of doors up, and as I approach, I see a tall, uniformed guy exiting the front door. At least *he* has a proper frown on his face. He's a good-looking sonofabitch, though, with broad shoulders and a no-nonsense bearing. But then he ruins the look by smiling at a little old lady who stops in front of him, asking, "Blake, dear, how is that lovely Sloane of yours? We haven't seen much of her lately. Is everything okay?" Her volume switch needs adjusting because she's nearly shouting.

It takes me a second, but then I process what she's saying:

Sloane? Could it be? *My* Anna Sloane? Nah, too much of a coincidence.

Hercules the Lawman enunciates loudly and clearly, "Everything's fine, Miss Alma. Sloane's at home with Grover watching over her."

Who the hell is Grover? This can't be my Anna after all.

But then the old biddy says, "I'm glad to hear it, Sheriff. I've heard lovely things about Grover—how he's remarkably polite. You sure took a shine to Sloane in a short amount of time, but I think when you know, you know."

"Yes, ma'am," he says all gracious and shit as he tips his hat and actually winks at the old broad. "Have a wonderful afternoon, and please tell Paxton hello for me." Obviously, he knows the old bird is hard of hearing, but what a two-faced creep.

"I'll give my Paxton your message. You know he went up to New York once, but he didn't like it much. I understand Sloane's from there."

"Yes, ma'am, Miss Alma. That place is an acquired taste, I guess. You take care now."

Sloane is from New York? It can't be that much of a coincidence. He steals my woman, and now he's keeping her captive with some henchman guarding her. Now I'm sure of it. I knew she wouldn't leave me for no reason; the babe is hot for me. She's my woman!

I recognize I must look like a schmuck standing here staring at them, so I quickly bend down to tie my shoe, only when I get there, I realize I don't have shoelaces, so I pull on my sock and I scratch my ankle instead. "Smooth" is my middle name, obviously. The sheriff walks past me at a good clip like he's in a rush. I stand and turn, noticing that he's armed. Then I see him duck into a local business, so I head back to the car.

I slam the door and announce, "We need to find out everything we can about the local yokel sheriff who just walked by. I think he's our connection to Anna." I direct Damien then, "Let's get outta town and find a place where we can sit and have a meeting with all four of us. We need to do a little reconnaissance."

Five minutes later, we're sitting in the empty bleachers of a deserted football field. I guess we're lucky that nothing's going on today. I pull up Google and search for "Honeybee Hollow sheriff." Bingo. I remember now the old lady called him Blake. His name is Sheriff Blake Ogden, and he hasn't been in this job for very long. Hopefully he's so new, he doesn't know what he's doing. I'm dying to find out where he lives.

"I think it's time to pay a visit to this guy's house. From the sound of things, it could be that Anna is there. I may be wrong, but it's as good a place to start as any. I want you two to tail him and figure out where he goes. But be discreet, you got me?"

"Whatter we gonna do if it's her, boss?" the guy we call Joey asks. The other guy is named Gianni, but we call him

Johnny Four Fingers on accounta someone got pissed at him and chopped off one of his digits a long time ago. Maybe he stole something. It's no big deal to me as long as he's not stealing from me.

"Well, duh. We'll take her. Whattya think we're doin' here? She might be in danger from that sheriff guy. He looked pretty mean, if you ask me."

"Smiling at old ladies makes you think he's mean?" Damien asks.

"Watch it, asshole. You're on thin ice. He's armed, and he might be intimidating Anna while he's holding her captive. He has some smooth-talkin' tough guy named Grover guarding her. I heard him say so. We gotta get her out of that place and back where she belongs. With me! Okay, let's roll. Damien and I will get us a place to stay tonight, and you two stake out the sheriff. When you find out where he goes, come meet us at the address we'll give you, and tomorrow, we'll all go get her."

I *knew* she wouldn't have left me on her own.

CHAPTER
Twenty-Three

I'm out back with Grover wandering around not too far from the house. I'm watching Grover become transfixed by a butterfly that's flitting around when I hear the sound of a car —no, two cars—coming down the gravel drive toward the house. It's not yet lunchtime, so it's not Blake, and it's too early to be Juni, so I'm suddenly nervous. I peek around the edge of the house and see… ohmygod. No! It looks like Sal with some guy and another car following them. I scramble back, lunge for Grover, and zoom back into the house. I set him down, lock the deadbolt with my key, and re-arm the alarm system.

Unfortunately, Grover hears the cars, so he runs off to the

front door to investigate. Wishing I hadn't set him down but not wanting to be seen or to take up any more time, I run and lock myself in the bathroom. Grabbing my phone from my pocket, I send Blake a text.

EMERGENCY! SAL'S HERE!

I don't get an immediate reply, and this has me spooked. Then I wonder if my eyes were playing tricks on me. Maybe it wasn't Sal at all. Maybe they were friends of Blake's, and I'm acting like a scaredy-cat.

The guys are at the front door now, and they're knocking and ringing the bell. This sets Grover off, and he's making a terrible racket barking at them. It sounds as if he's jumping up and down against the door. That sweet goofball probably thinks they want to play with him.

I stay put just in case it *is* Sal. My heart is pounding so hard it almost hurts. I wish I had Grover with me. Actually, I wish I had Blake, but Grover would do in a pinch.

Finally, the ringing and pounding stops, but I can hear voices heading toward the back of the house now. I recognize Sal's voice yelling, "Anna? You in there? We're here to save you!"

What the fuck? Save me from what? Come on, Blake! Answer me! Oh shit. These guys are at the back door now. It sounds like they're trying to kick it in, and I don't know how sturdy the door is. Then I remember what to do. I reach for the cord around my neck. I've worn it for so long, I forgot it was there. I pull it out of my shirt and squeeze the daylights out of the panic button. I can't hear a thing, so I hope it's working.

Grover is now having a conniption at the back door as the guys try to gain entry, and I'm so upset I'm about ready to puke. *Please, please decide I'm not here and leave*, I plead silently.

Sal continues to shout, "Anna? Is anybody named Anna in there?" over and over until I'm about to scream. But then two things happen in rapid succession. First, there is the sound of breaking glass and a loud clunk like a big rock hitting the floor, and then the alarm system goes off. It's deafening, and it's mixed with several loud voices arguing over each other. It's all so garbled, I can't even understand what they're hollering about. As if the cacophony wasn't already deafening, this is a whole new level of horrible—I can hear poor Grover whining at the bathroom door now. He knows where I am, and the poor puppy needs comfort, but if those guys get into the house, I sure don't want to unlock this door. Grover will give me away, and they'll know immediately where I am.

However, since I don't detect any new noises that seem to be coming from inside the house, I don't get the feeling that the men have gotten in. Maybe the alarm spooked them, and they left? I'm super happy that Blake has a keyed deadbolt. I imagine those jerks thought they could smash in the window, reach in and turn the knob, and just waltz in here. Hah! Quickly, I open the bathroom door, grab poor Grover, shove the door closed as quietly as possible, and relock it. I try to use my hands to cover his ears. Poor baby. He's shaking all over. Thankfully, he doesn't seem to have any glass in his paws.

Then the noise out there takes on a new level, and I hear an approaching siren on top of the house alarm. I breathe a sigh of relief, believing Blake's on the way. I wonder what happened to Sal and his goons, but I guess they lit out when the alarm sounded.

A minute later, the front door opens, and the alarm is turned off. "Sloane? Sloane! Where are you? Are you okay?" It's Blake, and I can breathe normally again. I open the door, Grover streaks out toward his hero, and I follow him on wobbly legs. I'm still making my way down the hall when I hear Blake cooing to Grover, "There's my good boy. Did you protect Sloane? Where is she, buddy?" I come into view and rush toward him. He wraps his arms around me so tightly I can barely breathe. It feels wonderful. I'm safe in his embrace.

"Where are they, Blake? I hid after I saw them, so I thought they might still be here after they tried to break in. I was so scared. It was Sal and maybe two or three other guys."

"I'm so glad you're okay. I was scared to death they had you. I had to make a split-second decision whether to come here and see if you were safe or follow the cars I saw leaving. I radioed the deputies a description of the cars and came here. Something in my gut told me you were alright. I don't even know why. It's like if you were taken by them, I'd have known it, and I'd have chased them down."

"How would they have known to come here? Who would have told them?"

"I have no idea, sweetheart. Maybe someone let something slip and they overheard, or maybe they bribed a resident for information. I hope that's not the case, but it could have happened."

"Why didn't you answer my text?"

"I was driving, and I couldn't chance it. I turned the car around, put on the flashers and the siren, and headed straight here. I was going too fast to send you a text."

"Makes sense. They broke a window to get in, and it set off the alarm."

"I'll fix it. We have to make sure Grover doesn't get cut, so let's put him in his crate with a toy and go assess the damage. I have extra glass in the garage."

We're cleaning up the mess when there is another knock on the door. One of the deputies is here. "I'm so sorry, you guys. It's like those cars disappeared into thin air. We couldn't find 'em anywhere."

"Damn. Well, they'll probably show up again. They seem pretty fixated on getting to Sloane." Blake turns to me and asks, "Do you think they saw you when they pulled up to the house?"

"It's possible, but I tried to stay out of sight when I looked around the corner to see who was coming. But if they had seen me, they'd have seen a brunette, so they might not have thought it was me anyway."

"True," Blake says. "But Sal also might have recognized you in spite of the hair." He turns to the deputy. "Thanks for trying to help. We'll send a description to the surrounding towns and see if anyone else spots them, but so far, the only crime they've committed is breaking a window, and that won't exactly be a high priority for anyone else. 'Potential kidnappers' sounds better, but we have no proof."

Just then, Blake gets a call. He answers and his eyes widen. "Fuck!" he hollers. "Thanks, I'll be there right away." He looks wildly at me and says, "Someone just threw a Molotov cocktail through the front window of Hot Stuff. There's a fire in Juni's coffeehouse." He grabs me and says, "Sloane, I can't leave you here. This might be a diversion to get me back to town and away from you, so the safest place is in the cruiser. He looks at the deputy and asks, "Ken, would you mind staying here and keeping an eye on things until we can get back?"

"Sure thing."

"If you need a snack or anything, help yourself to whatever you can find in the fridge. Read a book or watch Netflix. Hopefully, we can get back here pretty soon. Thanks a million." He looks at the dog crate where Grover is sound asleep. "You better let Grover stay put because of the broken glass. We didn't quite finish cleaning it all up. He'll be alright in his crate for a while."

Blake grabs a baseball cap for me as we run out.

WHEN WE GET BACK TO TOWN, BLAKE PULLS UP AS CLOSE TO Hot Stuff as he can get, but the fire truck is taking up a lot of real estate in front. Blake gets out and leaves me locked in the car, scootched down in my seat with the AC going and my hat pulled down low. I'm also wearing sunglasses.

He's back in less than five minutes, looking relieved. "Except for the broken window, the damage is pretty minor. Juni was just about to leave when it happened. She heard the crash from the kitchen and looked out to see the beginning of a fire on the table in front. Luckily, she keeps fire extinguishers handy, so when the firefighters arrived, she already had things pretty well under control. She'll need a new window and a new table, but the rest is just stuff that'll need some extra cleaning and some paint. If she'd left earlier, the whole place might have gone up in flames."

"How did the fire department know to come?"

"The owner of Shoo Buzz saw the guy hurl the firebomb through the window and called them immediately. He had no idea Juni was still in there, and he was scared stiff that the whole block of shops would burn down. The car the guy threw it from fit the description of one that Sal and his guys were driving."

"Can I check in with Juni? I want to make sure she's okay."

"She's pretty shaken up and wants to go home, but right now she's waiting on someone to fix her window."

"She needs company, Blake."

"And you need to stay safe from these bastards, Sloane. It's chancy enough just letting you sit here in the car in broad daylight. I can't let you get out and wander around."

"Yeah, okay. I get it. I'll call her then."

By the time I'm done apologizing for making a mess of things by being here in town and then doing my best to cheer up Juni, she has both Asher and Jack with her at Hot Stuff. I know she's in good hands with her guys, but I still feel responsible for the damage those creeps did to her place. It's her pride and joy.

Blake shakes his head and tells me, "I told her something might happen after she sent them on a wild goose chase for you. Those kinds of guys are ruthless, and this might just be the beginning."

The thought makes me feel like running away. I've brought way too much trouble into Honeybee Hollow. I don't know where I'd go, but it's beginning to sound pretty tempting to spare my friends any more grief.

We head back to Blake's place to relieve Deputy Ken. It's time to feed Grover too. He's had an eventful day and needs to blow off some steam. We quickly finish the glass cleanup job, then I go prepare his bowl of food while Blake takes him out and tosses a ball around for him for a couple of minutes. When they come back in, at least one of them looks happier. Blake sets to work replacing the broken window while I wonder what to do for dinner. I don't come up with any great ideas—probably because I'm too upset to eat.

Once he's full of supper, Grover conks out in his bed. He'll probably be out for a couple of hours, judging from experience. I help Blake clean up from his glass project, and we grab a couple of drinks.

Blake looks at the sleeping pup and then at me, saying, "I think I need to do something to work up an appetite for supper."

"What, like going for a run or lifting weights?"

He snorts. "Close, but no. I'm thinking more like some vertical exercises—the kind you do with a partner." He runs a gentle finger down my arm, eliciting a sigh from me.

"Ahh, I have just the thing," I tell him with a sly grin. I take his hand and lead him to the bedroom where I draw the drapes closed. You can't be too careful—we sure don't want an audience. I turn away from the window, and I'm startled to find Blake right there in my space—as if he can't be too far away from me suddenly.

"I can't stand the idea of what might have happened today," he says softly. "You're so special to me."

"Oh, Blake." My eyes suddenly brim over with tears, and he looks devastated by them as I say, "I should probably get out of everyone's hair and leave town before someone is hurt badly. This mess is all my fault."

"Never say that," he tells me firmly. "It's not your fault

you have idiotic parents who got you into a bad situation with a terrible person, and it's not your fault Sal hasn't caught a clue that you want nothing to do with him. You have a town full of people who care about you like family, and you didn't even grow up here. They all know you're a good person, and they want to help." He looks down and whispers, "But if you need to leave because you don't feel the same way about me that I feel about you, I won't stand in your way." His voice cracks on his final words.

"It's not about my feelings for you; I *love you*. It's because I don't want any more fires or vandalism or the serious kind of violence that might escalate into something far worse. I don't trust Sal for one second. He's ruthless and a hothead. He scares me."

"Then stay and let me protect you, Sloane. I love you, and I need you. Since you've been in my life, I've never been happier, and I can't go back to a half life of simply existing to do my job and pretending to be satisfied with the status quo. Let me prove to you how much I love you. You don't need to leave. We'll get rid of these guys. I have some ideas."

"What are they?"

"My first one is that I'm going to make love to you so well you forget you ever contemplated leaving my side. So let me help you out of these clothes…"

The next thing I know, our clothes are strewn all over the bedroom floor, and Blake is laying me across his bed. His large hands are everywhere, followed by his lips. I feel cherished and adored. There is no playful spanking this time, and I'm conscious of the fact that I don't need it either. I feel like I'm a goddess in his hands, and he is worshipping me.

He toys with my breasts until I'm dripping with need for him, but he makes me wait. He kisses down my belly and down my thighs, getting my hopes up and then dashing them away when he skips the part where I really want his hands and his mouth.

"Please, Blake," I moan. He chuckles in response as he lifts my leg and gives me chills when he kisses behind my knee. I stare longingly at his engorged dick, red-tipped and ready to take me. "Fuck me," I whine. "I need release." I reach for his dick, thinking I can stroke him enough that he's dying for me as much as I am for him, but he pulls just out of reach and winks at me as he sets my leg down.

"Patience, my angel."

"Kiss me then," I order him. But he doesn't change positions and give me his mouth. He does, however, get so close to my pussy I feel his hot breath on me, and my craving boils over. "Please," I moan.

"You know it makes me crazy when you beg for me, so I guess you're ready for a reward." He slides his hands between my thighs and gently opens my legs. "So pretty," he whispers with his eyes locked on my lady bits. He uses his hands to spread me wide open and gives me a long, appraising look that makes me want to squirm. Finally, *finally*, he lowers his mouth to me and licks.

"Oh, ooh," I groan. "Yes, that's it." But it's not quite it yet. I need more, so I tell him, "Harder, please!"

He laughs and firms up his tongue. It's better. And better, and almost… but not quite it.

"Blake," I sigh. "More."

I feel a finger slide into me, and I let out a long, relieved breath. Then a second finger slides in with it. I'm so wet for him it's almost embarrassing, but I know he takes it as a compliment. The man has to know I'm wild for him, even if I've threatened to leave town. I tense and release my muscles, enjoying the friction of his fingers and the firmness of his tongue.

At last, he's fingering me rhythmically, and he sucks my greedy clit into his mouth where he dazzles it with his tongue and sucks in and out, dragging me through his teeth. It's the best thing I've felt… since the last time we made love. He owns me—heart, soul, and body. My pussy may as well have "Property of Sheriff Ogden" tattooed across it because I'm spoiled for anyone else forever.

I feel the stirrings of an impending O bubbling to the surface. He must sense it too because he pulls back for an instant. I almost cry out "no!" but I see that he's just sucking his other finger into his mouth, and right away he's back, manipulating my clit to the brink of madness. I know the ecstasy is coming. It's coming! And then—*oh*! A large finger probes its way into my backside. I'm completely full of Blake. He's overpowering my sex, and I crash into a climax that elicits a long cry from me as I spasm and spasm through glorious pleasure. I see stars behind my closed eyelids, and the stars turn colors that streak and pulse. It's sheer beauty, but I still need more of him. Blake understands without me telling him, so he flips me over and slides into my soaking pussy. He continues to play with my sensitive clit as he starts to pump in and out. He's gentle for a while, crooning to me about how his life didn't begin until I came into it, and he loves me more than he ever knew he could love anyone. My heart melts for this beautiful man.

Gradually, Blake speeds up until he's pounding into me over and over, faster and faster. I'm still shaking with pleasure spasms from my last orgasm, but another one overtakes me as I feel him tense, ready for his release. With each of his massive thrusts I cry, "I. Love. You!"

Roaring like a lion, he spills into me and holds me to him in an iron grip that tells me he never wants to let go.

"Wow," I whisper. We collapse on the bed, panting and catching our breath. After a while, a thought occurs to me. "What were your other ideas, hmm?"

"Oh, uh… I didn't actually have any more after that one. I just really wanted to fuck you."

I roll my eyes and snort, but I get it. My crisis of conscience has been alleviated. For now.

"Okay, I really do have some ideas," he tells me in a sad voice.

"What?"

"We need to find you a safer place to live for a while until we can get these guys out of our town for good."

I gasp and sit up. "You want me out of your house?"

Blake wraps his arms around me, brings me back down to his chest, and answers, "Only because they seem to have a pretty good idea that you're here. You need to be safe, sugar bear, and I can't be here all the time. So we need to have you stay somewhere that they'd never look, but where there are people around. I hate not having you close, but I also have this crazy fear that they'll come and do something really terrible like light the house on fire to force you out of it. They already tried to burn down Juni's place just because they were pissed off at her. I wouldn't put it past Sal."

"What if they try to burn it down while we're gone, but Grover is here?"

"I'll start taking Grover with me to work. He'll probably enjoy it. And I'll set up some surveillance cameras that connect to my phone. It's the best I can do. I'd obviously hate losing my home to arsonists, but I also plan to start a rumor that you've left me for good. They might lose interest if the story is convincing enough."

I hate this idea… but I can't help but admit that it might just work.

B LAKE

O VER THE NEXT FEW DAYS, I'M AS EDGY AS A CAT. I'M SURE every car going down the street is one of the ones we're looking for, and each man on the sidewalk looks suspicious. The fact is, however, no one has seen hide nor hair of Sal and the Goons, which has become their unofficially official name. Aside from some deviously tricky moonshiners and continued shoplifting, there isn't a lot else going on crime-wise near us, so my deputies and I spend an inordinate amount of time trying to figure out Sal's next move.

Even without a lot of crime going on, I've had to hire another deputy so we can all have normal days off, and I finally found someone who seems promising. His name is

Rodney. He goes by Rod and gets along with the other guys great. Fortunately, he also likes dogs.

Other precincts in neighboring towns report that they don't have any suspicious new residents or visitors, but they promise to stay alert. The lack of sightings makes me wonder where these guys are hiding out and what they're planning to do—because I refuse to believe they decided to head home to New York. And since they don't even know if they were trying to break into the right house where Sloane is, they must be anxious for better intel.

There's a nervousness in Honeybee Hollow that we've never experienced before. It's like knowing there's an invisible pyromaniac nearby standing next to a powder keg with a cherry bomb in one hand and a box of matches in the other. Are the goons trying to make us think they're gone for good? Are they bringing in more men? Are those men more ruthless? Smarter? Better informed?

I lie awake at night trying to drive the worry out of my mind and *think*. Where would I go if I were a scumbag? It's hard to relate.

Since stashing Sloane away, nights are almost unbearable anyway. I've taken to allowing Grover to sleep on the bed just so it's less lonely. He thinks it's great, of course, but he misses her too; he looks all over for her in the house. At least he loves riding around with me in the cruiser or sleeping next to my desk in the office (I brought in his doggie bed since he wasn't using it at home). Birdie adores the pup, and she's been bringing him healthy homemade treats, assuring that at least one of us isn't miserable. Grover has fans all over town now, thanks to his friendly nature.

Since they're familiar with the area, my deputies Ken and Mason spend hours combing the surrounding county, checking out vacant or abandoned homes. There used to be more of these properties, but with the upswing of interest in Honeybee Hollow, people are buying up land and turning old places into nice vacation homes or places to live year-round. I was lucky to find my house when I did because there was a big increase in real estate sales that drove prices up shortly after I bought it.

There are several Airbnb and Vrbo rentals in the area, and some are investment properties owned by absentee owners, so I wouldn't expect to hear from them about a pack of mobsters living in their place. This makes finding these guys a little tricky if that's where they are, but Ken and Mason are going to tackle what they can find there too.

Betty at the Honeybee Hollow Inn is a nervous Nellie after the fire at Hot Stuff, and I can't blame her. She's called me twice when people checked in who made her jumpy. The first instance was a couple who had strong New York accents, but they turned out to be relatives of the pastor over at the Lutheran church. The second call was about a middle-aged man who checked in alone, and she thought that was suspicious. He turned out to be a building contractor from Lexington and a very nice guy. The day after he arrived, another man checked in with him, and they were seen around town acting quite affectionate with one another. That calmed poor Betty down. In fact, she went out of her way to recommend some places they could dine. Honeybee Hollow is a great place for lovers.

And through all of this, the whispers around town are, "What a shame about our nice Sheriff Blake and his girlfriend. She left him, and he doesn't know where she's gone. It's so sad because they seemed so happy. But you can never tell about out-of-towners. Maybe she had a boyfriend back home all along. Damn Yankees. Can't trust 'em."

Sloane is safely hidden in plain sight. There's the corporate camp outside of town that Asher manages; locals rarely go there since it's only open to corporate groups looking for bonding time.

Before moving in with Juni and Jack, Asher had a gorgeous little cabin on the premises that he remodeled into a real show piece. Even though it's sat empty for a few months, he hasn't let anyone else move into it—until now.

Sloane can get her meals in the dining hall with the corporate guests or privately in her cabin. When new "campers" show up weekly, she can pretend to be on the staff. She won't have a lot of interaction with them anyway because they're there for specific activities. The rest of the camp staff are under strict orders not to mention Sloane's whereabouts to anyone, including their own families, and if they do, it will result in immediate dismissal. Asher assures me they are a trustworthy bunch, so he's not concerned about loose lips. They're already used to not talking about business discussions they might overhear and all have signed NDAs. It's one of the selling points that help get big corporations to send their employees there for a relaxing team-building week.

It's probably the best place I could stash her, although frankly, I'd have preferred Fort Knox. Don't think I didn't consider it.

Asher reports back to me daily that Sloane mostly stays out of sight, but he's seen her take a few hikes around the property, and she's met up with Juni on those occasions because the property of their house adjoins that of the camp's. No one has paid any special attention to her, and when she's out, she makes sure to wear a hat and sunglasses. I'm nervous knowing she doesn't stay locked in her cabin, but everyone needs fresh air, and she also desperately needs her friend Juni. Asher swears that Paradise Pond, where the two women meet, is not a place the campers ever go, and their activities are closely monitored.

All Sloane and I can do is talk on the phone, and only when I'm at home. We can't let anyone know I'm communicating with her regularly because anyone could slip up and tell the wrong person, and that person could set off a chain of events that might result in an all-out manhunt for Sloane by the Goons.

Tonight, however, I'm feeling awful about sequestering her and think maybe we're going too far, and in the middle of that sorry thought, my phone buzzes with a call. It's Sloane, of course.

"Hi, Blake. You doing okay?" She always asks me if I'm alright, and that endears me to her even more.

"Not really. I miss you way too much, snookums."

She laughs and says, "Not *that* one, please. But I miss you too—like crazy. Do you think you could sneak out here for a while? The camp is isolated, and everyone left this afternoon. We won't have any new people until late tomorrow morning. It's just the few people on staff who live here, and the rest have all gone home for the night. I mean, who's gonna spill the beans? The horses?"

"I don't know, Sloane."

"Come on, Blake. You know I can make it worth your while…"

She has a point, and I can just envision her sultry look as she tempts me. Like a besotted fool, I cave. "I'll be there in about twenty minutes."

I'm so stinking paranoid I check my mirrors probably more than I look at the road in front of me on the drive over to the camp. Luckily, I know these roads like the back of my hand by now. There isn't any traffic, so by the time I get there, I'm more jittery with excitement than with worry.

Sloane opens the door stark naked, and I think my heart stops for an instant. She has softly lit the cabin with a few candles, and I feel like I'm walking into a dream. As soon as the door slams behind me, I can't grab her to me fast enough. I wrap myself around her like a blanket. My possessiveness for this woman has notched up to a new level of crazy. Wordlessly, I kiss her until our lips are swollen.

She takes me by the hand and draws me over to the big bed. It's enormous, so Asher clearly designed it for his own comfort. I briefly wonder what kind of bed he created for Juni, Jack, *and* him to "sleep" in at their new house, but all thoughts of Asher are banished when Sloane starts to take my clothes off. She kisses me wherever she exposes bare skin. I can't stop petting her and nuzzling whatever is closest to me. Every inch of her is precious to me.

Once I'm as naked as Sloane, we fall into the bed, still kissing and caressing, but Sloane seems bent on being the aggressor tonight. She pushes me onto my back and fondles her way down to my junk. I'm ready and willing for anything, but after a couple of delicious strokes up and down on me, she leans over and engulfs me with her hot mouth. I strangle out a cry of lust, "Yes, oh yes." She starts to go to town on me as I grab a fistful of her glorious hair and hold on for dear life. Just when she thinks—and she's right—I'm about to explode in her mouth, she pops off with a naughty grin.

"Sit on my face, beautiful. I need you," I croak at her, and she readily complies. She's musky and wet—so responsive as I devour her slick pussy. Within a couple of minutes, she gives a long, deep moan, and her body tenses. Her face seems transfixed as she shudders with ecstasy. Gently, I coax her down my body and impale her with my lonely dick. *Ahh.* Just what I needed. "Show me how much you love me, Sloane."

Slowly at first, she slides up and down on me effortlessly. She's soaking with my saliva and her own juices. Gradually, she speeds up, and her delightful tits bounce up and down, giving me a wonderful show. I reach up to play with them, caressing and pinching her rosy nipples. The candlelight makes everything more sensual than usual. I feel as if there is music playing, but it's only in my head. The reality is that I hear our own sex sounds. Nothing is better than this.

Faster and faster Sloane rides me, and I'm so near coming, but I need her to be with me, so I pull her off, flip her over, and impale her again. I have one hand on her breast and the other on her clit that I manipulate just the way she loves it.

"Come with me, darlin'," I command as I pound into her heavenly body.

"Spank me!" she cries, so I let go of her nipple and give her one resounding smack on her bottom. That's all it takes. She hollers, "Yesss!" and her whole body contracts, squeezing the cum right out of me. I roar with delight and relief, and together we make so much of a racket, we're probably scaring the animals in the forest around us. Finally, we collapse panting on the bed.

"I'm so glad you talked me into coming," I tell her. That sets her off in a fit of giggles, so I amend my statement, "Coming over here to see you, I mean."

Before I fall asleep and do something dumb like spend the

night, I suggest a shower, so we head into the gorgeous bathroom that Asher also designed. It's incredibly beautiful with a walled garden just outside the glassed-in shower so it feels like you're showering in the Garden of Eden.

Sloane explains, "Asher made this whole thing. The outside wall around the garden is secured with a locked gate. He uses the gate to bring his gardening equipment in from his shed and not drag anything through the cabin. But the wall provides total privacy for the shower, and on hot days, it's fun to open the sliding glass door and feel like you're showering outdoors. I think Juni and Jack had him design something similar for their house because they liked this so much. Anyway, he told me that sometimes when he needs a break, he comes over here to putter in the garden, and if it's lousy weather, he just relaxes here until he has to go back to work."

"Wow, I wish I could see the garden in the daylight." Then I remember something. "I forgot to tell you. Tomorrow, I have the dog trainer coming over to work with Grover and me first thing in the morning. That ought to be interesting; the trainer seems great. His name is Hayden Thiele. We've talked a lot on the phone, and it turns out he used to work with K-9 police dogs before he set up his own business. Grover's pretty good on a leash, and he's mostly cooperative, but he's terrible when I try to get him to sit and stay, and his 'down' command is nonexistent."

Sloane sighs and answers, "One more thing I'll miss. I hope you guys enjoy it though."

"I'm sorry. We'll get things figured out soon, I hope. I can't tell you how badly Grover and I miss you."

"Yeah," she whispers. "Soon."

Leaving her there is hard, but a couple of hours later, I have to go. I don't want to be seen in the light of day leaving the camp for no apparent reason, but I can't keep making up more lies either.

I drive away, vowing that I'm going to redouble my efforts to find these guys.

As it turns out, I don't need to.

CHAPTER
Twenty-Five

BLAKE

GROVER IS IN TYPICALLY HIGH SPIRITS IN THE MORNING, SO I play fetch with him to try to wear him out a little. He loves it. I have the whole day off to devote to him, so maybe we can take a long walk on one of the wonderful hiking trails around here after our session with the dog trainer. Hayden said he'd be here around seven. He must be an early bird too—or he has lots of places to be today.

When someone knocks on the door at a quarter to seven, I'm not too surprised. I guess he overestimated the length of time it would take him to get here.

But when I flick on the porch light and open the door, it's to find the last person on earth I expect to see on my doorstep

—especially at this early hour. Salvatore Caputo, in the flesh. He has a smarmy grin on his face that I'd like to wipe off with my fist. And maybe he'd swallow a few of his teeth while I'm at it. I've only ever seen him from a distance, but up close he's slightly more impressive than I expected. He's strong-looking in the way a boxer looks fit and coiled to lash out. I see the scar on his chin that Sloane described to me and the diamond in his ear. He's several inches shorter than I am, but he's built like he's powerful and knows how to throw down. Every muscle in my body immediately tenses up as I glare at him.

"What do you want?"

He starts to step inside, but I get in his way, keeping the door only partially open. There's no way I'm letting him into my home, and I don't want Grover running out to greet him. "I thought we could have a friendly chat about my Anna, Blakey-boy," he answers all smooth and oily sounding.

"I don't know anyone named Anna, and it's Sheriff Ogden to you." I wish I had my gun and cuffs on me. I do, however, have my phone, so I stuff a hand in my pocket and surreptitiously tap the back of my iPhone to start it recording sound. I have no idea where this conversation is going, but if he pulls out a gun and shoots me, at least there will be proof. "So what do you want to discuss, Sal?" I emphasize his name.

He scoffs. "Anna, Sloane, whatever you wanna call her. I thought we might clear the air about *my* fiancée. You need to know a few things, Sheriff." At least he's learning how to address me. "She told me some things this morning."

This morning? Suddenly, my blood chills and my heart stutters. *How can this be*? I don't ask him what she said though. He's probably bluffing. I hang onto this hope until he says, "She told me she'll go back to New York and get hitched just like we'd planned, and she's done with you. She saw this town and had a little fun, and now she's finished here. So I want you to lay off because she was mine first. And if you try to follow us or sic anyone on us, I'll kill your whole damn family faster than you can say, 'Honeybee Hollow.'" Apparently, he finds his own words hilarious because he cackles joyfully at his cleverness. "Anna told me how devoted you are to your mama, and that old bird would look pretty great with a gunshot hole in her head, now wouldn't she?" He adds ominously, "I know her address."

It's the graveyard a few towns over to the west, asshole.

I narrow my eyes at him, wondering if this is just some weird thing he made up to get under my skin or if Sloane told him all of this to misdirect him, and she knew I would see through it. My guess is it's her way of saying she isn't going along with his plans to marry. So I tell this jerk, "You leave my mother out of this, Caputo." It's another way of confirming on the recording who I'm talking to. "And how do I know you've spoken to this supposed fiancée of yours?"

"Look Deputy Dawg, you may think you're smart, but you're as wet behind the ears as they come. We've kept a close eye on you and know you paid a midnight visit to do a little boning last night. I know a man has his needs, just not with *my woman*. But thank you for letting us know where she was hiding."

I think I'm going to throw up. I led these creeps right to her. "Are you tracking my car?"

He's full-on guffawing now. "Well, duh! We've known every time you've moved that car three feet. And I must say, you lead a very dull life here in Bumfuckytucky. Do you ever do anything more interesting than help old ladies across the street?" I glare at him, but he carries on, "I'm just here to give you a polite warning. Stay away from Anna, and her life will be safe and protected. Come near her again, and not only will I put a bullet through your mother's skull, I'll ruin Anna so badly no one will ever want her again, *capisce*? And her dumbass father will never know it was me, 'cause I might just get rid of that asshole too once we're all set up nice in business together." He lets that sink in a second, and I can't understand why he's telling me all of this. "Maybe old man Sloane will have a 'heart attack.' Those can be arranged pretty convincingly when you know how. But *you* also have to understand that she's coming home with me of her own free will. She don't like it here all that much. Says it's too quiet for her tastes. She likes some action, ya know? You shoulda seen her when I gave her a gun to play with. She got so hot, I thought she was gonna climb me like a tree." I have to restrain myself from slugging him into tomorrow as he adds, "We both know she's some kinda sexy beast."

He turns to go but adds, "I mean it, dumbass. Don't go

near her again. She's already heading outta town with my guys, so there's nuthin' you can do now anyways. So don't go calling your buddies to put a tail on us, and if you follow me… well, let's just say, you're not gonna be able to follow me." He cackles and starts to walk away—the cocky bastard, but I quickly reach inside to the table by the door and snatch up Grover's leash. I lunge for Sal and loop the leash around his neck. Pulling tight, I simultaneously sweep his feet from under him and have him on the ground in less than two seconds. I hold him down using more pressure on his neck and a knee to the middle of his back. He scrabbles around with his hand, and I see he's going for a gun, so I grab the weapon before he can reach it.

I'm restraining Sal and telling him his Miranda rights as a truck drives up, and a guy hops out wearing a shirt with a Thiele's Dog Training logo on it. I call out, "Hayden!" so he's aware who knows him here.

Hayden assesses the situation immediately and asks, "How can I help, Sheriff?"

"It would be great if you could run inside and grab the handcuffs I left on the kitchen table."

He's back in seconds with Grover on his heels and offers me my service revolver along with the handcuffs. "Thanks. Hold onto the gun for a second while I cuff this sack of shit." I get Sal's hands restrained and haul him into a standing position, even though he's hollering that I'm assaulting him for no reason. Then I unceremoniously drag him over to my squad car where I start to shove him into the back seat.

Sal starts thrashing and screaming his head off like a meth-addled toddler having a temper tantrum. "Not in this car! Don't put me in here! Stop, please stop!" I eye him suspiciously.

"Is there something wrong with taking a ride in my cruiser down to the station so I can stick you in a cell?"

"You don't understand! This was all Damien's idea! I was a patsy the whole time. You have no reason to book me! At least take me out of the car so I can explain!"

"Right. Only I have lots of reasons to book you. Arson, kidnapping, threatening an officer of the law, possibly attempted murder, I'm guessing an unregistered weapon… But we'll see about that in a second. I'm still going to have you sit in here anyway while I give the car a good look."

Sal continues to thrash, scream, and blubber about how he has responsibilities and he's too young to die, and blah, blah, blah, so I have a pretty good idea of how he was planning to get me out of the picture. I give my car a swift perusal and spot the bomb stashed in front of the rear passenger side wheel.

Not wanting to blow up my car (though I wouldn't lose much sleep over blowing up Sal, since he obviously put the damn thing there), I call for assistance. Deputy Mason is trained in explosives, so I fill him in, and he says he'll be here in about five minutes.

I need to get to Sloane in the worst way. I can't imagine any of what Sal said is true about her wanting to leave, but the possibility of it still makes my heart hurt. I also hate the idea that those other idiots who work for Sal might have her with them.

It seems so typical, considering what I know of Sal, that he would want to boast about his connection to Sloane and brag to me before blowing me to kingdom come. Pompous ass. Well, the joke's on him now.

For the next couple of minutes, Sal continues to holler about everything while Hayden and I let Grover get acquainted with him. Hayden has a firm yet friendly rapport with the pup, so I see good things coming out of this association. I desperately want to leave though. I excuse myself a moment and call Ken and Rodney, asking them to go over to the camp to see what they can ascertain there. Obviously, I can't drive my vehicle until it gets de-bombed. Finally, I hear sirens approaching and breathe a little easier. Mason has also alerted the fire department. Good man.

Mason sees exactly what the plan was for the bomb and defuses the situation quickly and efficiently. As soon as the car moved forward, it was going to trigger the bomb and set it off, and I would have ended up looking like charred confetti. Mason also tells us, "It had enough explosives in it to take out not just your car, but your whole house too." Good lord.

"Can we move this jerk into your car so you can get him into the holding cell, and I can get over to the campground where Sloane is supposed to be—if they haven't already taken her?"

"Sure thing," Mason says. We proceed to move Sal—who's still kicking and screaming—out of my car and into Mason's while Hayden tries to keep Grover from getting too excited. It takes longer than I'd have hoped. Hayden offers to follow Mason back to the office in case he needs help moving Sal out of the car and into the holding cell. It may not be proper protocol, but I have no fucks to give about that at this point.

Before they leave, I call out, "Hey, Hayden, you're deputized!" That oughtta do it. He gives me a quick salute in acknowledgment. I like this guy.

Then I root around for anything attached to my car that looks like a tracking device and find one stuck just inside the wheel well. Shaking my head, I put it in the house—it's evidence, after all—grab Grover, harness him up, and head out toward the camp with my flashers on and siren wailing.

CHAPTER

Twenty-Six

SLOANE

AFTER BLAKE LEAVES, I FALL INTO THE DEEPEST, MOST wonderful sleep I've had in weeks. I lose all sense of time passing, so when I hear a knock on the door, it jars me awake and I wonder if Blake forgot something. I have no idea how long it's been since he left, but it's still dark out, so it can't have been that long. I don't bother to check my phone for the time. I'm pretty convinced it's either Blake or Asher, but why Asher would show up before dawn is beyond me. Anyway, I open the door, wearing only one of Blake's big comfy t-shirts and a sleepy smile.

Uh oh. Big mistake. If I weren't half asleep, I would have had more wits about me, but as it is…

Three burly men swarm in shoving me back asking, "Are you Anna Sloane?" I'm still blinking my eyes awake, and I can barely remember my name… either of them. Two of the guys grab me by the arms, and the other holds a photograph up and looks at it and then looks at me alternately a few times. "Hair's different, but it's her." He says in a no-nonsense voice.

Crap! I took out my contacts to go to sleep. My blue eyes are obvious. There's nothing I can do about that now.

"Sal says you're coming with us."

"Sal's here?" I ask in order to stall them. I remember from somewhere that stalling is always good. Or was it stalling is always bad? Oh, hell if I know. I'm still groggy, and these guys are pissing me off.

"Sal's handling other business, but we're here to take you to him. He said you'd be happy to go, but if you aren't, we're supposed to convince you." He smiles at me, but the look seems so foreign to his face, it's scary.

"I see." I'm starting to wake up more, and it's all beginning to make sense now. "I'd love to see Sal," I tell them with a sugary smile and using all of my acting skills, "But he'll be really angry if I show up like this," I indicate the extra-large Honeybee Hollow Sheriff's Department shirt I'm wearing. "So can you give me a few minutes to spruce up a little and put on clothes?" Please say yes, *please* say yes! The men hesitate, so I add, "He'll probably be real mad if he finds out you saw me like this, too."

"Awright. Ya got five minutes," the biggest one says. He definitely seems to be the one in charge here.

"Oh, it takes me more time than that to put on makeup, and I know how particular Sal is about my appearance."

"Okay fine, lady. You can have ten whole fuckin' minutes to make yourself presentable to the boss. But not one second longer. Got it?"

"Yessir. Thank you." They let go of me, and it's a relief to be out of their clammy mitts.

I go to the chest of drawers and pull out some random clothes, socks, and underwear. Then I grab my shoes and rush into the bathroom. As fast as possible, I pull on the clothes and shoes and turn on the shower. Let them think what they want. I grab the key to the gate and step around the falling water. As quietly as possible, I slide the glass door open and step out into the garden. I close it and head for the gate. The lock works smoothly, so I'm past the wall in mere seconds. Unfortunately, I can't relock from this side, so I pocket the key and take off at a run. I pray the sound of the rainfall shower is enough to mask what I've been doing, but I know I have to get out of here and far, far away from those guys. I head for the trail I think I remember, but with no sunlight or flashlight, I'm pretty confused. There's only a sliver of a new moon, so I'm in pitch dark. Dawn could be hours away for all I know. I squint at trees and rocks looking for familiar landmarks, but nothing looks the same as in daylight, so I just hope my instincts are correct. I pray that I'm heading toward Paradise

Pond which is close to Juni, Jack, and Asher's house where I can get help. But I might be heading in the opposite direction. I just keep telling myself to run, no matter what. Get away from those horrible men.

I keep running and running until I get a stitch in my side and have to stop and take some deep breaths. I listen for any approaching sounds, but all I can detect are regular forest noises, and *ouch*! Mosquito bites. Yuck. Asher warned me to be careful of them out here, and he said they were at their worst after the sun goes down. At least I was smart enough to put on long pants instead of shorts—even though it's hot and sticky out here. I swat at the bugs landing on my arms.

Onward. I have zero desire to see Sal Caputo again as long as I live. He is truly a disgusting person.

It occurs to me that I might be leaving footprints for anyone to follow, so I start to do crazy stuff like stepping on rocks until I slip off of one and clobber my knee, ripping a hole in my jeans. Great. Stick to the grass or dirt. I keep running until I'm all run out, and then I keep walking. I notice, however, that the terrain is changing, and the path is getting steeper. I'm not heading toward Paradise Pond at all. It's flat there. Well, nuts. It's all going to be easier when the sun comes up, I just know it. I'll be able to figure out where I am. Keep moving, keep moving.

I'm thirsty. I wonder where the stream is. I should have come to it by now.

I decide I can run some more.

Is that a glow on the horizon that I can barely see through the trees? Is it nearly dawn? Wow, these trees are really big. I can barely see any stars because of the density of the forest.

What was that? It sounded like an animal—kind of screechy and growly. People don't make noises like that. I hope it wasn't a bear. Are there bears around here? What am I supposed to do if I come across one? I know they can climb trees. I hope I'm not screwed.

After running and walking until my legs are about to give out, I figure it would be okay to take a little rest. Also, I need to pee in the worst way. Shoulda done it when there was indoor plumbing, but I didn't want to take the time. May as well go. I find a low branch I can sit on, use it like a chair, and… ahh, relief finally. Too bad there's a shortage of TP, but I'm afraid of grabbing leaves. I have heard of poison ivy, but I have no idea what it looks like, so I'm not about to risk that. I shudder with the thought. It occurs to me, not for the first time, that I have been brought up to be the ultimate city girl, and that kind of pisses me off. I think if I knew more about nature, I'd really enjoy it. I pull up my pants and find a drier place to relax a bit. It is getting minutely lighter, but it's still terribly dark.

I trudge around until I find a nice sized boulder. I find it, of course, by stubbing my toe on it and almost pitching forward into it face-first. That would have *hurt*.

Once again, I strain my ears for the possible sounds of people following me. I hear no footsteps and no voices, so for now I take that as a good thing. However, as my breathing slows and the color of the sky that filters through the trees begins to go from ebony to a pinkish gray, it also occurs to me that I am irrevocably lost.

What have I done? Maybe it would have been smarter if I'd tried to hide in the kitchen or the barn.

Too late now.

CHAPTER
Twenty-Seven

B LAKE

O N MY WAY OUT TO THE CAMP, I GET A CALL FROM A SHER, and my immediate thought is, *This can't be good.*

"You need to get out here right away," he says by way of greeting. "Is Sloane with you by any chance?"

"No, and I'm already heading to you. Aren't my deputies there?"

"Damn! They're here and they've both been shot. Paramedics are on the way."

"Fuck! How bad?"

"I dunno. Lots of blood though, and they're both unconscious."

"Is there any sign of Sloane?"

"Well, yes and no. I'll show you when you get here. Gotta go. The EMTs are here."

"Two minutes." I disconnect, and I want to puke so badly right now. Someone shot my deputies! They're good men with families! Colossal rage burns through me like molten glass.

A minute and a half later, I scream into the camp and park as close as I can to the cabin. I leave the AC on for Grover and run toward the carnage. The sight is grim, but the men are alive. One is already being hoisted into an ambulance, and the other is nearly ready to go. There's blood everywhere, just as Asher said.

I rush to him. "Tell me what happened," I demand.

"Sloane usually gets her breakfast in the dining hall early in the morning before most of the campers are up, but today she was a no-show. I decided to head over here to check on her. That's when I found the deputies. I called 911 immediately and then went inside to see if she was in there—hoping she hadn't met the same fate as your guys. The place was empty, and there's no blood anywhere, but here's where it gets pretty weird. The shower was running, but the water had gone completely cold, so it had been on for a long, long time. Your shirt was laying on the floor, so I wondered if you'd been here or if that was just something Sloane liked to wear. I looked around a little and realized the key to the gate wasn't on the hook where I normally keep it, and then I noticed the gate was ajar by about an inch."

"Are you saying you think Sloane escaped from those guys?"

"That's kind of how it adds up to me, but who knows? And where did she go if she ran out of here? She doesn't seem to be around camp, or she'd have shown herself after the ambulances arrived. Also, no one sleeping or preparing breakfast heard any shots, so the shooter must have used a silencer."

"Oh, God. First, we need to find those clowns and see if they have her, and then we need a search party to find her if she's still around here. Or maybe she'll find her way."

"Blake, there are bears, copperheads, and all kinds of dangerous shit out there, and she isn't at all prepared for how to handle herself in the mountains. I just hope she followed a path she's familiar with and will come back on her own. If she was smart, she just ran and hid, but if she panicked, she kept going. And since she's not back by now, they either took her or I'm afraid she might be lost."

"Fuck! I need to organize a countywide search for those creeps," I tell him, but my instinct is to run through the woods looking for Sloane.

THE NEXT HOUR OR SO IS TORTUROUS. I MAKE SEVERAL CALLS to set up a statewide manhunt for Sal's henchmen. Knowing they are suspects in the shooting of two deputies makes everyone take notice, so the level of cooperation is terrific, and I know roadblocks will be arranged immediately. But I also desperately need to know where Sloane is and what's happened to her.

I've never been so scared in my life, and I realize that Sloane *is* my life.

Birdie at the sheriff's office, Juni at Hot Stuff, Betty at the Honeybee Hollow Inn, Buford at The Hive, and Jack at his gallery Imagine all pitch in to alert everyone they can that Sloane is somewhere—probably near the camp, but she may have been transported away by bad guys. Everyone is asked to be alert for anything that looks suspicious and to be careful because the men are armed and dangerous. They reassure everyone that Sloane never actually left, she was just hiding from a malicious man who is now in custody. Once again, a group text goes out to all of the merchants so that everyone knows to be alert, stay safe, and to continue spreading the word so that everybody knows exactly what's going on. Within minutes, the whole town is on high alert.

Asher is invaluable. He knows the area well and knows how to handle a lost hiker situation, so he takes it upon himself to organize a search party. We even have a helicopter and pilot standing by if we need him. Volunteers begin to show up at the camp, including Hayden who is now accompanied by two huge bloodhounds for tracking.

"Deputy Mason had already left to come here, so I put the prisoner in the custody of a guy named Levi Spencer. Birdie vouched for him and called him 'sergeant' when he said he wanted to help out any way he could. Since he walked in with a cane, I thought trekking through the woods wouldn't play to his strengths. I introduced Sal to him and explained that if he gave Sergeant Spencer any shit, the guy had permission to shoot him." Hayden laughs. "You should have seen the color his face went. I thought he was going to piss himself. Anyway, I didn't want to just leave that creep with Birdie in charge of him. What is she, ninety?"

Well, that was thinking outside the box. "I believe she's eighty-something," I tell him. "She's as tough as nails though. Thanks for showing up with the dogs and dealing with Sal. And that was a good call. Levi is a former Army sharp-shooter."

"Happy to help. I was worried the other guys would sneak in and try to spring Sal loose, so at least he's under armed guard this way." He pats one of the dogs. "Hap and Hazel live for this stuff. When can we get going?"

"Right away," I say, feeling a bit of relief. "Do you think I ought to bring Grover?"

"Sure. He can learn from the big dogs, and he knows Sloane, so that could be a big help. Now, can you show the hounds a piece of clothing she's worn recently? Or maybe her pillowcase or something?"

I go get Grover out of the cruiser and let the dogs sniff each other. That goes well, so I take them into the cabin and look around for where Sloane might have kept her dirty laundry, but then I see my shirt. "She was wearing this when I left her last night. It was washed after the last time I wore it."

"That'll work." He lets each of the dogs, including Grover, have a good long sniff. Hap and Hazel immediately go into work mode, but Grover just looks happy to be playing a game. He is a puppy, after all. His tail is wagging his whole body, he's so excited.

A little while later, we leave a couple of people back at the cabin to search around the campground with Deputy Mason. I take off behind the dogs with Hayden, Asher, Skyler—who grew up here and knows the area as well as anyone—and Skyler's dad Mike Colfax, another native. It turns out Mike's parents used to own the land the camp is on, so he really ought to know his way around.

Asher and I have two-way radios, and he's equipped with a first aid kit and insect repellant that we all spray ourselves with. He furnished us with plenty of water to carry, and we discussed taking horses but agreed Sloane didn't likely get that far away in a couple of hours. If it *has* been a couple of hours —that's just an educated guess. My supposition is that Sal's men went to get Sloane around the time he showed up at my house. Also, I have a pretty good idea when the deputies showed up here, and she probably didn't leave long before that.

If she left alone. We still don't know for sure.

We all agree to head out armed with rifles. Each of us is

former military, law enforcement, or an experienced hunter, so we all know how to shoot. And we know when not to shoot.

Hazel and Hap work perfectly together, and after circling around the area for a while—no doubt following places Sloane went recently—they zero in on the most recent scent and take off in a straight line toward a path that heads into the woods. Either this is a favorite path Sloane takes on her daily walks, or they're really onto her trail. At one point, the dogs split up, but soon they're working in tandem again, so I think there might really be a fresh trail. Grover seems pretty excited about bugs and animal scat we pass, so I'm hoping he gets back with the program. It's hard for me to tell whether he's out here for fun or has a scent in mind. I guess time will tell.

About an hour and a half into our trek without much of anything promising, I get a radio message from the state troopers. At one of the roadblocks, a car matching the description of the one driven by Sal's men was seen approaching at an ultra-high speed. The officers moved out of the way, fearing a collision, but someone in the oncoming vehicle opened fire. No officers were injured, but they returned fire on the vehicle.

At this point, my heart just about stops. *Was Sloane in that car?*

But it gets worse.

The tires got blown out, and the vehicle flipped several times. They came to rest in a gulley where the troopers found all the passengers and the driver dead.

Now I start to shake. Violently. And then I hear the rest of the words. "There was no indication that your girl was in the car, Sheriff. It was just three men. From their IDs, the deceased were identified as Damien Nardo, Joseph Pastore, and Gianni Prizzi."

I have to sit down on a rock. Skyler immediately comes to my side and looks at me questioningly. "Are you okay, buddy?" he asks.

I close my eyes and nod. "They didn't have Sloane. She's still out here somewhere. Now they're all dead except for Sal —that is, unless there were more guys working with him. Anyway, I need to get it together and get back to work."

"Alright then." Skyler gives me a friendly cuff on the back. "Let's go find her!"

I redouble my efforts by calling out periodically, "Sloane! Where are you, Sloane?" Then I look at Grover and tell him, "Find Sloane." He smiles at me the way dogs do and wags his tail.

CHAPTER
Twenty~Eight

I'm exhausted, and I feel like a dope. I've gotten myself lost, and I'm so thirsty I can't even spit—not to mention I'm covered in bug bites that are driving me crazy. It's time to come up with a plan. *Think.*

If I could find a stream, I could follow it, and maybe it would take me back to the pond near camp. The problem is, I don't hear any water running, and I don't see any evidence of a stream. I sniff the air. What does water smell like in the woods? Certainly not like the Hamptons—or the Jersey Shore. That smells more like pizza, popcorn, and corndogs anyway with an overriding smell of salt water. And saltwater taffy.

Damn, now I'm hungry. I look around and wonder what's

edible. Who am I kidding? I'd probably eat something poisonous and die an excruciating death from killer berries, deadly mushrooms, or some stupid thing. I've never even been camping, but I've always wanted to try making s'mores around a campfire. Stop thinking about food!

How could I go through life and not develop *any* survival skills? I can strut around in high heels and ride the subway at rush hour, but I can't figure out how to find my way back to camp.

Footprints! I must have left them. I hop off my rock, making my knee hurt, and search around for anything that looks like my tracks. The ground is either pebbly here or covered in plants, though, so I'm not immediately picking up on anything. Besides, I'm still not sure I wasn't followed, and maybe running right back to those creeps isn't the wisest move.

I strain my ears once again, listening for anything out of the ordinary. All I hear is a lot of buzzing insects and plenty of birds with the occasional squirrel chittering away. Cheeky little show-offs. I bet they have lots of food. *Stop it*!

I sit back down on my rock and burst into tears. I'm ashamed of myself, both for being lost and for crying. Crying makes me feel weak and ridiculous, so I force myself to *cut it out* immediately. How can I make tears when I can't even spit? I scoop a tear off my cheek and stick it into my mouth. Gross. That was dumb. My hands are filthy.

I don't know why a man as brave and wonderful as Blake

would ever want anything to do with me. I'm pathetic. No wonder my parents never had any use for me until Sal came along.

Suddenly, I see movement in the trees ahead, and I almost faint from fear. It's them! The scary dudes with guns have found me! I drop down and hide behind my rock. Hearing nothing, I wonder if they're going away. Oh, I hope they didn't see me. Slowly and carefully, I rise up a tiny bit to peek over the top of the rock, praying I don't get the top of my head blown off. There is still movement out there, but it's silent. Oh, thank God. It's a herd of deer. Does and fawns from the looks of them. I fall sideways onto the ground and start to laugh manically. My noise startles the deer, and they run off. They're so graceful and elegant.

I'm relieved they weren't bad guys or bears.

It occurs to me that maybe the deer will lead me to water, so I stand and look in the direction they went. It's as if they vanished into thin air. "Thanks for nothing, guys," I mutter to them as I strain to see anything. I'm not wearing my contacts, so while my distance vision isn't terrible, it's also not the best. Just another way I messed up by not putting them on, but I sure didn't need to take time doing more than I did when I escaped from those creeps.

Even though I can't see the deer, I reason that they had a plan when they took off in that direction, and I'm intolerably thirsty, so I head off in their direction with a new sense of purpose. The trees are thick here, so I'm dodging them as I zigzag around them and suddenly stop dead. I smell something. Smoke? It doesn't smell like a fireplace or a bonfire, but something is definitely burning. Intrigued, I forge ahead until I see a small plume of smoke up ahead. I'm not looking at where I'm going when my foot slides, and another smell assaults my senses.

"Ew!" I cry as I look down and realize I stepped in some kind of poo. It's large and gross and probably pretty fresh. At least it's not as stinky as dog doo, but it sure made a mess of my shoe. I hate the forest. If I get out of here alive, I ought to go back to the city where I belong.

But then I think of Blake, and another tear rolls down my cheek. If he still even wants me, I can't leave him. I hope I stay alive long enough to see him again. I manage only somewhat successfully to wipe the mess off my foot in a patch of grass and continue on toward the smoke.

I see a flash of color up ahead and realize it's some kind of vehicle. Well, that's pretty promising! A vehicle means there's a road, and someone had to drive it here. Maybe they'll give me a ride back to the camp. The closer I get, the smell of the smoke begins to bother my eyes a little. It smells like burning plastic. *Ugh.* I slow down and take in the sight before me.

Two bedraggled, bearded men in faded bib overalls and no shirts are sitting on beat-up chairs next to some kind of Rube Goldberg contraption that is emitting the foul smoke at one end. There are a couple of wooden barrels off to one side. I instantly think of the men on that *Duck Dynasty* TV show several years back. While those guys were nice, these men seem way rougher, but I don't want to judge them on sight. One is dark haired, exceptionally tall, and skinny as a rail. His straggly black and gray beard extends almost to his waist. The other is short and pot-bellied with a bushy, flaming red beard. As I creep closer, I step on a dried branch, and it makes a loud crack. Instantly, I'm looking down the barrels of two shotguns, and the men have menacing expressions. I do not want to cross them.

I throw my hands in the air and cry, "Don't shoot! I'm lost, and I need your help if you'll be nice enough to… uh… not shoot me. Please?"

The taller man lowers his gun and squints at me. His buddy still has his gun pointed in my direction, and I don't like it a bit.

"I can pay you… some cash… later. I don't have anything with me here, but I can get it to you somehow or… uh…" I don't think I'm getting through to them because neither one has answered. Their eyes keep flicking around past me like they're looking for something. Maybe they think I'm here with friends.

Finally, after glaring at me for a couple of minutes, Round Guy asks, "You alone?"

"Yes! I told you I'm lost. I need to get to town or the camp or the main road—just out of this forest. Can you take me or give me directions? Please?" Then I see they have a large jug of water and a couple of tall cups next to them, and I ask,

"And could you spare me a drink? I'm absolutely dying of thirst."

At last, the redhead drops his gun and mutters something to the tall guy I can't hear from this distance. The tall one smirks and says, "Sure, honey. Come on over. We'll give ye a drink an' show ye the way to deliverance."

That seems like a funny way of putting it, but if I don't get some water in me soon, I'll pass out, and their jug looks crystal clear and refreshing. I drop my hands and approach them slowly and steadily, so they know I'm not trying to threaten them in any way. "I'm not armed," I reassure them, but the only response I get to that is a loud snort.

"Looks like ye found yerself a bear," Tall Guy says looking down at my foot.

I gasp, "That's what it was?" I swivel around to see if any bears happened to follow me and then realize how dumb that sounds. Why would a bear follow me… unless it's really hungry. Do they eat people?

"Black bear," he answers. "It ain't eaten meat lately, or that'd stink to high heaven." He guffaws at my expression. Then, acting more like a gentleman than I expected, he steps aside and offers me his chair. "Set yerself, honey, and I'll getcha that drink."

"Oh, thanks." I plunk myself down and try to get comfortable. The chair is rickety, but it's at least better than sitting on a rock.

I watch as he uncorks the jug and fills his cup about three-quarters full. I'd sure like more water than that, but maybe he's afraid of spilling it. It surprises me, however, when instead of handing me the cup, he takes a drink from it first. He looks at Round Guy and smacks his lips. "Best yet, Cletus. This 'n's granny-slappin' good." Cletus smiles at this weird statement, and I see he's missing a front tooth. These guys look like they belong in a movie about hillbillies.

"Yessiree, Buck," the round red one says.

Looking at me thoughtfully, the man I now know as Buck says, "Ye sure is a purty thing. Here ye go. Take a small sip at first. Be careful." He hands me the cup.

I've always wondered why in movies they tell people to take a small drink of water when they're obviously dehydrated. It's always seemed so dumb to me. So instead of following his useless instructions, I guzzle a huge swallow and keep chugging down gulps until… ohmygod I think I'm going to burst into flames.

Gasping for breath, I choke out, "That's not water!"

"*Water*? 'Course it ain't. It's the finest moonshine in Kentucky. What'd ye think we's makin' here?"

I swivel my head around—making myself dizzy—and realize belatedly this must be a still, now that I'm… My vision goes black as I drop the cup. The last thing I'm conscious of is smacking my head on something.

CHAPTER
Twenty~Nine

I AM TREMENDOUSLY ENCOURAGED. THE DOGS HAVE COME across some great evidence that Sloane is out here and nearby. We found a spot where she may have relieved herself, and we discovered some thread fragments and a light smear of blood where she must have smacked herself against a rock. I bet that hurt, and I hope it's not serious. The discouraging part is that she's not answering any of my shouts as I holler her name over and over.

The dogs push on until we find a footprint in a big pat of bear scat. It looks like a woman's shoe by the size, and all three dogs are fascinated by it. We also see where she tried to wipe the scat off of her foot a few feet away.

The dogs press on, and I pull the lid off my canteen and gulp down a big swallow. *Poor Sloane*, I think. She doesn't have anything to drink. I'm glad we have extra water for her when we get to her. It's so stinking hot today.

We trudge onward for a while when suddenly Grover starts barking his head off and wagging his tail. It's unmistakable. He knows where Sloane is. "Good boy. Find Sloane," I tell him, and Grover takes off on a dead run. The other dogs give chase, and we do our best to keep up. We come over a small rise and see a sight I certainly was not prepared to face today.

"GROVER, NO!" I scream, and then, "GROVER, COME!"

Two moonshiners stand side-by-side with their shotguns trained on my puppy as he barrels toward them. All Grover knows is his Sloane is there, and it's his job to get to her. He remembers the game.

"DON'T SHOOT HIM, PLEASE!" I bellow for all I'm worth and then try to persuade Grover back to me. The best I can do is get him to stop running. He sits on his haunches and whines. I look at the moonshiners and see now that they have their guns trained on me. However, my companions are just now catching up to me, and each of them cocks their rifles and points them back at these characters.

"No one needs to get hurt. Put down your guns, please. I won't arrest you if you just let the woman come to me." I can barely see her behind the two men. One of them is particularly wide, and he's blocking my view. "Sloane, can you come here, please? Tell these guys you're with me. We promise no one will get hurt." *Why isn't she talking or moving?*

I recognize these two. They are the slipperiest fucks in Harlan County, and I've been trying to arrest them for years. But I have my priorities. "Look, guys, let her get up and we'll leave you alone. You have my word. I'm Sheriff Blake Ogden from Honeybee Hollow. We just want the lady so we can get her home safely."

"We knows who y'are, Sheriff. It's nice of ye to offer clemency, but this lil' lady a yorn ain't movin'."

I place my gun on the ground, so I look like I mean what I say, and advance on them. "Why not? What did you do to her?"

"Jus' gave her a friendly drink is all. She complained she was parched and downright begged for a swallow," the one I know of as Buck answers.

"What proof is that stuff you make?"

The fat one, Cletus, says proudly, "Judgin' by the bubbles in the shake test, I'd say one-twenty proof or thereabouts. At least."

"And you let her drink it straight? You could kill her with that rotgut!"

As quick as you can blink, Cletus has his gun aimed at my heart once again. "Take that back. We ain't makin' no rotgut. This here's *fine* moonshine."

"Sorry, sorry. I'm sure you're right and it's great stuff. Just put down your gun and let me get to her. She might need medical attention." I pray she isn't blind or already dead. She isn't used to this kind of alcohol, and I'm sure she was dehydrated when she swallowed it. If it wasn't distilled properly, it could easily poison her.

"Eh, awright," Buck answers. "She ain't no use to us in this here condition anyways. Get her outta here and off'n our hands. She's as drunk as Cooter Brown." He must have had a snort or two because he seems awfully mellow. He and Cletus step aside.

I shove my way to Sloane who is leaning over the arm of the chair in a weird position. I'm followed by Grover who immediately bestows kisses all over her face. She'd probably be grossed out by all the doggie spit if she knew about it, but she doesn't react. I feel her pulse and realize it's erratic, and her skin is cold and clammy.

"Asher," I shout, "We need that helicopter. *Now*."

"Already on it, Blake. I gave them the GPS coordinates, and he'll be here in a few minutes. The only trouble is that he won't be able to land in all these trees, so we'll have to put her into a basket. It's risky with the canopy of branches. She could get caught up in a tree."

"They's a bit of a clearin' 'bout a quarter mile thatta way," Buck offers helpfully. "We, uh, had a little fire a while ago. Hop in the back a the truck, and we can take y'all."

I look at Asher who's already communicating with the pilot again. "I let him know we'll have better coordinates soon," he assures me.

"Thanks. Let's go." I scoop up Sloane into my arms, and all of us pile into the back of the ratty old truck. I fervently hope Buck is telling the truth. Once we're on our way, I see that Skyler is pouring out a drink of water for Grover and telling him he's a hero. Grover laps up the water and licks Skyler's face while Skyler scratches his back, making Grover's tail wag like an out-of-control metronome.

I cradle Sloane to me hoping I can tell her about this scenario soon.

We bounce around for what feels like eternity but is probably only a few excruciating minutes before we come to the edge of a burned-out patch of land in the forest. They had to have worked awfully hard to put out the blaze before it became a major forest fire, so I have a bit more respect for these men. When we hop out, I can't help but ask Buck, "How come this whole area didn't go up in flames?"

"Aw well, we had the area pretty well cleared 'cause this's where we was harvesting our firewood in the first place. But we keep fire extinguishers handy too. Don't want to ruin the forest, ye know? It was just some little stuff that burned here."

"I see. Well, I can't thank you enough for bringing us here, but I have to at least ask you to stop moonshining because it's my job. For now, anyway, I'm going to forget what I saw today."

Buck cackles. "Sheriff, the spot you jus' visited has already been moved. Our lookout partners saw what was going on too. Good luck findin' us again."

I don't doubt a word of what he's saying. They may be breaking the law and trespassing on government land, but they did me a solid, even if they did potentially poison Sloane in the first place. I don't get the sense they did it maliciously, and they helped get her rescued quickly. Tomorrow, I may feel differently. Anyway, I hear the chopper approaching and see the truck bouncing away in a cloud of dust.

There's enough room for two of us in the helicopter with Sloane, so when Skyler and his dad swear they know the way back, and Hayden says he and his dogs thought this was a romp in the park and will have no trouble getting back, Asher turns over his backpack with the safety supplies to Hayden, saying, "Just in case."

They also take our rifles, and I'm briefly sorry to be weighing them down, but we sure can't have the rifles when we get to the hospital. I pile into the helicopter with Asher and Grover. Sloane is already inside strapped to a litter.

Thirty

BLAKE

As soon as we touch down on the helipad on the roof of the hospital, Asher puts out the word to Juni and Jack where we are and that we have Sloane.

Sloane is whisked away to the ER, and I make sure Grover isn't going to disgrace himself before taking him indoors. He's amazingly calm, having just had a noisy helicopter ride. I'm so impressed with this dog. He pees on a bush and poops on command, so after I scoop it all up in a bag and toss it, I figure we're good to go.

Asher and I head in to discover Sloane has been taken to have her stomach pumped. I fill the hospital personnel in on everything I know about her particulars, and we're sent to the lounge to relax and wait for news.

Relax… right. I'm wound up tighter than a drum. I'm terrified of the aftereffects of homemade alcohol and what lasting repercussions it could have on her. Some of that stuff is downright nasty, and we have no idea what additives are in it. Moonshine is illegal not just because selling homemade alcohol interferes with Kentucky's all-important bourbon trade, it's also dangerous for people to drink.

When one of the nurses—or whatever she is—looks at Grover disapprovingly, Asher announces with a scowl, "The dog is here on official law enforcement business."

No one is kicking Grover out of this hospital.

I leave him for a moment with Asher so I can go wash my hands.

Asher is a calming influence, and there's almost a spiritual air about him at times. I've never fully appreciated his demeanor before today. He looks like a Samoan warrior, but he is a gentle, capable voice of reason who brooks no nonsense and takes no shit. As we wait for news of Sloane, he speaks to me about how much he knows she loves me and tells me my devotion to her is beautiful to see.

Our friends begin to join us. First Brooke arrives, then Juni and Jack come in holding hands.

Brooke reports that Levi is enjoying his day as a fill-in deputy overseeing his dangerous charge. "Apparently Sal never shuts up and has been complaining about everything from 'inhumane' confinement to his lousy lunch. He was demanding to see a lawyer, but he hated the public defender who showed up and told her to get lost. She was all too happy to oblige. Anyway, Levi asked me to bring him his guitar and has spent the day making up songs about jailhouse blues, bad guys who end up hanging from a rope, and just generally yanking Sal's chain." She laughs softly. "I took Levi a delicious boxed lunch from the deli, and it cracked him up when Birdie handed Sal a plain Velveeta sandwich on white bread and an apple. Levi thought Sal was going to throw it at him until the jerk realized that was all he was going to get. Birdie says the prisoner is going to be transported over to the Harlan County Detention Center in an hour or less. But Sal says he has a hotshot lawyer who's going to get him off as soon as he gets here from New York, and furthermore—let me make sure I get this right—'Everyone in Honeybee Hollow is a stupid hick.' Charming guy."

Throughout all of this story, I can't help but notice that Brooke is not looking her best. She looks a little peaked, if you ask me, and every so often, she rubs her huge belly and grimaces.

"Brooke, are you feeling okay?" I finally ask her when she's done with her story about Levi and Sal.

"Oh, uh, yeah." She leans in and says quietly, "I'm kind of in labor, though. I'll just wait until Skyler and Levi can get here to let anyone know."

Juni looks at her with her eyes popping, "What do you

mean you'll 'wait'? If that baby's coming, we need to let your guys know and get yourself checked in. I mean, you're already here in the hospital."

"Exactly. I'm here, so it's perfect. It's my first baby, and from what I've read, they take a long… ooooooh. Um, uh oh." She grimaces again and looks down. We all look where she's looking and see a growing puddle expanding around her feet. "Whoopsie."

Juni takes Brooke by the arm and propels her toward the admissions desk while Asher calls Levi. Jack calls Skyler, who luckily seems to be back in an area with cell service now.

Thirty minutes later, the waiting area is teeming with friends and concerned neighbors. The news of Sloane's reappearance has ignited a town-wide prayer chain that she'll be alright, and the news of a new baby causes more friends to come and share the joy. Levi finally makes his way in, asking to see his wife immediately. He looks half crazy with worry. I know how you feel, buddy. He is whisked away by the attendant who is all too happy to tell him Brooke's already in a delivery room.

Finally, someone comes to get me, just as I see that Skyler has also arrived, demanding to see his girlfriend, Brooke Spencer. The same attendant at the desk looks taken aback, but she checks Brooke's file and responds with a quizzical look, "Yes, I see that you *are* on the delivery room list too. Please come with me."

We head down a hallway, following our respective leaders,

but after a few moments, we split off, heading in opposite directions. "Thanks for everything today, Skyler," I tell him. "Good luck in there. And congratulations."

"Thanks, Blake. I really hope all is well with Sloane. This has been some day, huh?" He strides off through a set of doors.

I'm taken into a patient room, and I'm relieved to see Sloane lying in the bed. She looks both beautiful and awful at the same time. Her eyes are closed, so I don't know if she's sleeping or awake. Her arms and face are covered in scratches that I didn't even notice before and the tell-tale red welts of multiple insect bites. She's also hooked up to an IV and a couple of monitors that are beeping rhythmically. I go immediately to her side, and Grover hops up onto the bed to snuggle in beside her. It makes my heart swell when I hear the soft sound of a laugh coming from her. "There's a good boy," she whispers with a bit of a slur and reaches to stroke his head.

I'm about to say something when Dr. Ahluwalia comes through the door. I've always liked her. "Hey, Blake," she says. "I understand you and Sloane have had quite the adventure."

"That's one way to put it. How is she doing?"

"She's dehydrated and worn out, and she was suffering from mild alcohol poisoning. She was extremely inebriated when she first arrived, but the effects of that are wearing off. We purged what we could of the offending moonshine out of her stomach and are pumping her full of fluids, so she'll be just fine, except for a tender throat for a while. I don't mean to downplay the seriousness of any level of alcohol poisoning, so we should all be thankful you got her here so quickly. The only other thing we need to watch for at this point is West Nile virus, considering all the mosquito bites she has. You both need to be vigilant for a couple of weeks. If she's been infected, she could show no signs of it at all, or she could have flu symptoms for a few days—lethargy, achy joints, or vomiting. Worst-case complications can be serious though, so I want you to call me if she develops a high fever or serious rash—anything that's out of the ordinary. Right now, we'll just treat her with antihistamines for the discomfort. She can probably go home the day after tomorrow so we can keep an eye on her and continue the IV fluids. Any questions?" She reaches over to pet Grover's shiny head and gives him an ear rub, and now I'm certain I like this woman.

"No, thanks, Doc. I think that covers everything." I want so badly to be alone with Sloane.

"Thanks for keeping our town safe, Blake. I understand we were infiltrated by some rather shady characters for a while. And from what I gather, it's been a struggle."

"All taken care of," I say with a nod and sit down next to Sloane. I take her hand, and I'm gratified to notice she's no longer cold and clammy. She just feels like Sloane. Grover lets out a sigh of contentment and stretches.

Dr. Ahluwalia lets herself out saying softly, "Best of luck to both of you." She smiles, and she's gone.

"Are you disgusted with me?" Sloane asks. Her voice sounds like sandpaper, so I offer her a drink of water. She takes a sip and says, "Thanks."

"I'm not the least bit disgusted with you. Why should I be? I love you, and I'm more relieved than I can say that you're alright."

"I made a mess of everything, and then I was dumb enough to get lost and cause everyone all this trouble…" She looks about ready to cry, so I lean over and kiss her lightly.

"Hey, you did the right thing by running away from those guys. They shot at our deputies and state police, and there's no telling what they'd have done to you if you hadn't escaped. And, yeah, things got pretty crazy, but you'll be okay. We'll have to talk about it when you're ready, but you can save your throat for now."

She opens her eyes wide for a moment and then starts to laugh. She clutches her throat and coughs. Laughs some more and then a tear rolls down her cheek. "I'm ridiculous." Only it sounds like "radiculush."

"No, you're perfect. I'm a lucky, lucky man you came into my life, Sloane, and now that you're in it, I hope you'll never leave. When I was worried that you'd been taken by the mob, or that some danger would befall you out in the forest, or that you were poisoned by those crazy moonshiners' brew, I knew life would never be the same without you. You're it for me, and that's all there is to it." She stares at me, so I continue. "While I certainly don't need today's level of excitement all the time, I also know that I need you in my life, and I hope you'll stay here forever. Will you, Sloane? Will you agree to stay and be mine as long as we live?"

"I might be loopy, so I can't be sure, but that sounded something like a proposal."

"That's exactly what it is. If you want, I can do it again properly with a pretty ring when you're stone-cold sober, but I just wanted to let you know that you mean everything to me, and I'm serious about this. I've never been so scared about anything as I was of losing you."

She closes her eyes a moment, opens them, and it dawns on me that I'm looking into her true blue eyes. Eyes I never hope to see covered with brown lenses again. "Okay, Blake. I promise to be yours." She giggles. "In that case, will you be my date for the Fourth of July celebration? I hear Levi is going to sing the national anthem again." Her voice fades out almost completely by the end of all that.

I give her a huge smile. "Of course, pookie." She grimaces at me, and even I have to agree that nickname is *not* a keeper. "Oh! You just reminded me. Levi, Skyler, and Brooke are having their baby. Right now. They're in delivery."

"Cool!" Her eyes droop again, and she asks, "Do you mind if I take a little nap now? I'm kinda worn out."

"Go ahead. We're not going anywhere, although I will have to get Grover home in a while to feed him. He was your rescuer, you know. He found you. Well, he had some help from Hap and Hazel, who are a couple of amazing bloodhounds Hayden, the dog trainer, owns…" I realize by her breathing she's asleep, so I sit back and feel the tension in my body dissipate. It's the most relaxed I've felt in weeks. I can fill her in on everything all in good time now.

The door opens, and I look up to see Juni grinning ear to ear. I put my finger up in the shushing sign and tilt my chin at Sloane, so she knows Sloane is sleeping. "She's going to be fine," I whisper.

"Wonderful news!" She pumps both fists in the air and adds in a stage whisper, "And Brooke just had a baby boy! Samuel Colfax Spencer."

CHAPTER
Thirty-One

After my release from the hospital now that I'm definitely stone-cold sober, we're sitting side-by-side on the couch when Blake asks, "Should I call your dad and ask his permission or his blessing for us to get married?"

"While I appreciate your manners and understand why you'd ask, I don't care what my father has to say about the matter. He showed me he has no regard for my well-being or happiness by trying to sell me to the Mafia so he could make money with their involvement in his business. He probably ought to be arrested just for that. And if that isn't enough to prove he's a scumbag, I've also had a lifetime of being shoved aside and ignored by my parents, and it hurt. So, no. Please let's return the favor and ignore them. I don't honestly care if I ever speak to them again. And I sure as hell don't need them at our wedding. I can walk down the aisle unaccompanied or have one of our friends escort me."

"I understand." He nods but looks pensive. "But they did house you and make sure you got a good education at least, didn't they? That ought to count for something, right?"

"They sent me to boarding school when I wanted to be at home with them. They never called me or showed up for school functions even though it wasn't far away, and then I got myself a scholarship and worked all the way through NYU. So while they paid for my early education, I always felt it was more a means to get me out of their hair. College was all my responsibility because my father said he was done paying for me."

"Okay, I get it. I'm just worried that someday you might regret not having contact with them. I grew up without any family, and I have often wondered how life would have been different if I'd had one. Still, I know that not all families are worth it merely because you share DNA. There has to be some reciprocal love or at least respect, and from what you say, your parents haven't displayed much of that."

I'm glad he gets it, but I add, "Blake, I'm used to having no contact with my parents because they ignored me for so long. They were never there for me and only showed an interest in me when it benefited them. No contact will feel like normal, unfortunately. I'm much more interested in building a family with you and doing it the right way."

"Believe me, I know how it feels to live in a house with people who barely tolerate you through no fault of yours," he says with a sad expression. Just then, Grover comes over and lays his head on Blake's thigh as if he knows Blake needs some extra affection. The sweet dog gazes up at Blake like he hung the moon. Blake smiles and looks at me with unmistakable love in his eyes. "Having our own family would be amazing."

A couple of days later, Blake makes good on his promise to propose to me properly with a beautiful ring, flowers, and a candlelit dinner at the Honeybee Hollow Inn's restaurant. He's even a little nervous, which is cute and endearing.

Betty is beside herself that her inn is a part of this momentous occasion, and the other diners clap and hoot when I say yes. How could I not? I'm only promising to spend my life with the sweetest, sexiest, most handsome man alive, who has proven he'd move mountains for me.

There was never a doubt in my mind that I'd say yes, of course. Once I got it out of my head that I was some kind of bad luck charm that swooped into this wonderful little town and messed things up irrevocably, I was alright. The outpouring of love from friends has made a huge difference.

The buzz about what happened with Sal and his goons is

not dying down quickly. The fact is that stories about the Mafia coming to town to nab the sheriff's woman will keep the gossip mill going—possibly for generations to come.

Levi says he's working on a ballad about it. He's calling it "Never Mess with a Hollow Man."

I'm glad Blake and I didn't try to start the rumor that residents of Honeybee Hollow are called "Mooners" because my run-in with moonshine left a distinctly bad taste in my mouth. I don't need a reminder of that experience. In fact, I haven't been too interested in drinking anything alcoholic. Maybe I'll eventually enjoy a nice glass of wine again, but for now, water, juice, and coffee are all I need.

While we were not able to plan a June wedding in the town's gazebo, much to the dismay of Bea at Honey Bea's Blossoms, we do plan to have a fall wedding in our backyard. The colors in early October will be splendid, and we love the idea of having it at home. Levi is going to sing with his band. We'll get married in the early evening, have a huge supper for everyone as the sun sets, and then we'll dance until everybody is worn out.

"I wonder if Banger the Wildflower Whiskey drummer will keep his shirt on at a wedding," I muse. "I've heard he gets hot and likes to fling it at people."

"I've seen him do that. Are you hoping he does or doesn't?" Blake asks.

"I haven't decided." He gives me a mock frown. "Hey, if I

want to ogle a great-looking man, I always have you, Blake. I'm just curious."

Birdie—who cackled at me, "I told you he'd come around"—has taken it upon herself to organize volunteers to help out with cooking and decorating, and Skyler's mom Tracy enlisted her Sewing Bees to design a dress for me. Her comment was, "We haven't had such a great opportunity to shine since Tanner and Zoë Lassiter got married years ago when he was mayor. That was great fun, and we're all even better at sewing now." This made me cry; what a wonderful group of ladies. They're like the extended family I've always wanted.

We are overjoyed that Deputies Ken and Rodney will make a full recovery. They're both doing well, but Rodney has decided to retire and take up a less potentially dangerous job. I guess being wounded so badly was terribly difficult for him as well as for his wife and kids. He's decided it would be wise to go into the family auto repair business with his dad and his brother—as his father had wanted him to do all along anyway. I hope it works out well for them. Ken, on the other hand, said, "This isn't stopping me. I doubt we'll see too many more mobsters in town."

Blake is in the process of hiring more deputies, and he's being extra careful to find the right fit.

When I'm not involved in planning the wedding, the rest of my summer is taken up with following through on creating a community theater. I'm not surprised that there is a lot to accomplish. The kids who have heard about it are excited. Parents are happy for their kids when I tell them I'll be holding after-school acting classes for various age levels, and even more thrilled when I say I'll also have adult classes. In the winter, we'll have auditions for a variety show that we'll put on next spring. While I do plan to make money from teaching the classes, the proceeds of ticket sales will benefit the high school. They generously offered their auditorium, so it's only fair. My hope is that charging for classes will make the students take their performance seriously, but if a talented prospective actor can't pay, I'll make arrangements for that as well. Local businesses have offered sponsorships and plan to advertise in our programs. This will help raise money for props and costumes. It's going to be a great community project.

Juni ended up permanently hiring a couple of the ladies who were filling in for me while I was in hiding. They both loved the job and the constant connection with the patrons. I miss working at Hot Stuff, but I still see Juni and Brooke as often as possible—several times a week. They are the greatest girlfriends anyone could ever have. And oh my… little Sammy Colfax Spencer is the cutest baby ever. He looks exactly like Levi, and I'm afraid he's giving me baby fever.

About six weeks or so after my hospital stay, I start to feel absolutely dreadful. I can barely keep my eyes open, and I'm woozy all the time. I've thrown up a few times, but honestly, I would sort of welcome the relief if I could do it more regularly—only barfing doesn't actually give much relief. I've tried to hide my symptoms from Blake, so he won't worry, but he's all engrossed in hiring and training his new deputies anyway. He's been out of the house extra early and home late every day this week, so it hasn't been too hard. I've been sleeping late, and I usually feel somewhat better by the time he gets home at night. But I'm so miserable, I decide to get an appointment with Dr. Ahluwalia. I'm sure I have West Nile, and it just took this long to manifest itself.

However, when I begin to explain my symptoms to Dr. Ahluwalia, instead of looking worried for me, she breaks out into a radiant smile. *What the heck*? She reaches into the cabinet and hands me a cup. "Sloane, please just head through there to the bathroom and bring us a urine specimen, would you?"

On my way home, I reflect on the jumble of events during the days surrounding my fleeing through the forest and subsequent hospitalization. I guess I must have missed a few pills. Maybe even quite a few.

I wonder how Blake will take the news.

On a whim, I take a detour to the Hollow Five and Dime and wander around until I find what I think will work. Then I call Blake. "Hi, I don't mean to bother you, but will you be home at the normal time tonight, or will you be late?"

"I won't be late. Things are calming down. Is everything okay?"

"Yep. Peachy. I just miss you, that's all."

"That sounds promising. Maybe I'll make it earlier than usual."

"I'll have your favorites ready."

"For dinner?"

"Eh, maybe."

"Even better. See you in an hour, *mamacita*."

Oh, you have no idea. "Wonderful. I love you."

As soon as I hear Blake's car pull in, I pour him a beer in a sparkling new glass mug. I grab a water for myself and set them down on the kitchen table. I greet Blake at the door, basically accosting him by throwing my arms around him and kissing him breathless. When we both finally come up for air, I say, "Congratulations on your new job."

"Huh?" Blake frowns with confusion, so I hold the mug up to him with the etched message facing him. His expression clears as he reads, "Promoted to Daddy." His eyes light up then, and he whispers reverently, "No way! Are you sure?"

"Absolutely. I was afraid I had West Nile virus because I've been feeling awful, so I saw Dr. Ahluwalia today. She confirmed it had nothing to do with mosquitos. Then it dawned on me how many pills I must have missed, and it all made sense. Are you happy?"

"You have to ask?"

"Just checking. It's not like we're married yet." I can't hide my smile, no matter what my words sound like.

"Who the hell cares these days about that?" He takes a swig of beer and grins. "Oh my God, I love you. Sloane! We're having a baby! Have you told Grover yet?" he laughs.

We're both laughing.

The dog comes wandering in just then, looking extremely silly in a t-shirt printed with the words "Best Big Brother in the World" across his back. Grover goes over to Blake and tries to rub the shirt off on his leg. I take pity on him then and pull it off, and Blake scratches his back for a while, setting off a tail-wagging extravaganza.

Blake swallows more of his beer and announces, "We need to celebrate, sweet mama. I hope whatever you planned for dinner can wait." He takes me by the hand and whisks me through the house to the bedroom.

"Blake?" I ask as he starts to remove my clothes.

"Huh?"

"All I planned for dinner was DoorDash. Later. I wasn't too sure when we'd get around to eating."

"That's my clever wife-to-be and mother of my child. Ooh, look! Your tits are bigger," he says as he hefts them in his large hands. "How did I not notice that? Mmm." He engulfs one of my nipples into his mouth, and I shiver with delight.

Blake's still fully dressed, so I say, "Sheriff, you're not going to search me, are you?"

His eyes light up, and he raises his eyebrows. "Are you hiding any contraband on your person, you naughty woman?"

"I'll never tell. You'll have to see for yourself."

He quickly whisks my shorts off and grins at the lacy red thong I'm wearing. "Pretty," he says, but it's also history within seconds. "Alright… spread your legs, ma'am." He tries to sound serious as I widen my stance, but the twinkle in his eye lets me know how much he's enjoying this game. "I need to perform a cavity search." And wow, his finger slides into me so fast my head is spinning. I'm as wet as can be. He pumps in and out of me for a while, and I can't hold back the moans. The whole time he's prodding me, his thumb is caressing my clit, and I'm embarrassingly close to getting off already. So when he adds a second finger and nibbles on my nipple, I can't stop the pleasure that crashes though me.

"Yessss, oh yeah. So good, um… officer," I moan as waves of delight pulsate through my body over and over. "More, Sheriff. Please!"

"Get on the bed near the side, ma'am, ass up, and keep your legs spread."

"Are you going to search *more* of me?"

"I have to be thorough, ma'am. It's the law."

While I'm positioning myself in the most vulnerable position there is—butt in the air and completely exposed, Blake is quickly unzipping his pants and reaching for the lube beside the bed. I'm so turned on, I have to keep fingering my own clit, but when he sees me, he says, "Oh, no you don't. No possible tampering with the evidence." Crack! His big hand smacks my butt cheek, and I instantly orgasm again. The sound that comes out of me is positively primeval.

"More, pleeeeze!"

Crack! The other cheek is now involved, and I can't help squirming.

"Hold still now. I have to proceed with my search." He quickly lubes up my hole, then plunges a finger into my ass at the same time as he reinserts one into my pussy.

Oh, it feels so good. And I'm coming again.

He's pumping in and out, and I get a sudden flash of what my friends who have two lovers must feel like, but it fades when he says, "You are the most perfect woman in the world, Sloane—my wife-to-be, and you hold my heart in your hands." He's broken character but made up for it in spades with his sincerity.

His finger leaves my backside, and he shoves his steely dick into me. I welcome the delicious burn for a few seconds, and he begins to fuck me. Slowly at first, then faster and faster, deeper with each stroke. My fingers manipulate my clit harder and harder while his finger is in and out of my pussy making squishy, wet sounds. It's wild and carnal, and I cannot get enough of this man. He alternates his invasion of my body with a thrust of his hand, then a thrust of his dick. I'm going wild with pleasure, and my legs begin to shake. I start to feel orgasm number I-don't-remember-how-many beginning when Blake bellows, "Sloane! Oh God, Sloane!" and he thrusts everything he has into me like he's burying himself inside me, and hot spurts of cum jet into me over and over. Nothing can top this. Finally, his quaking body stills, and he leans over me to kiss my neck. "I love you so much," he whispers, and I hear a hitch in his voice. Apparently, he's as overcome with emotion as I am.

His spent member slips out of me, and he straightens. I feel his eyes on my body, so I hold my position. He strokes my bottom with both hands, and I can still feel a slight burn on my cheeks as he admires his handprints. He runs his finger through a dribble of cum that's running down my inner thigh. "You make me feel like a caveman sometimes," he says with humor in his voice. "Don't ever stop."

Blake pulls back and proceeds to remove his uniform, so I flip over to enjoy the show. I can never get enough of watching him reveal his body. His dick is still swollen and glistening wet, and I imagine how happy it must feel as his pants drop to the floor. He peels off his shirt, showing me his defined muscles that I love to run my fingers over. He is truly magnificent.

And he's all mine.

"Did you already feed Grover?" he asks.

"I did."

"Excellent, then let's take a little rest for a while. I'm hungry, but we can eat later. I'll be right back."

He's back with a warm washcloth in seconds and tends to me carefully. I pull down the bedding and crawl in as I hear him washing up back in the bathroom. Once again, he returns and snuggles in next to me. Within moments, we're both asleep.

About an hour later, I wake up from a deep sleep to realize Blake has positioned his face between my legs. The duvet is gone, and his hands are all over me. He tongues and sucks me to yet another delicious climax before sliding up my body and entering me. His erection is titanium, and it feels perfect as it fills me up. I can't help the purring sounds of contentment coming out of me.

Missionary sometimes gets a bad rap. It's actually wonderfully intimate, and it allows for kissing at the same time as fucking. I wrap my legs around him then, and Blake demonstrates my theory perfectly by fucking my mouth with his tongue in the same rhythm as he's boning me. Soon he's emptying more of himself into my greedy body with a massive groan and nuzzles his face in my neck. Perfection.

After lying there in peaceful quiet a while, enjoying the

feel of his weight on me, I stroke up and down his warm back and say, "We probably ought to feed you. You need more protein after this evening's activities."

"Probably, but you're building a whole new person, so you need to eat even more than I do. I'll go grab us some menus and my phone." He wanders away stark naked, and I'm happy to watch.

I know I'm the luckiest woman in the world.

CHAPTER
Thirty-Two

Summer has burned itself out, and it's now glorious October—meaning that our wedding day is finally here. I am ridiculously flattered by the way the town has turned out to celebrate our happiness. Everything looks incredible. At least three hundred guests have arrived, bearing gifts and food, and the area is a fall fairyland of autumn colors, flowers, and twinkle lights.

I guess I shouldn't be so surprised about the number of people who showed up. We had sort of a combination bachelor and bachelorette party at The Hive the other night, and that place was crawling with people—so much so they had to line up outside and wait for people to leave so more could come in.

Fire regulations, of course. Wildflower Whiskey played for hours, and Buford Wallace, the owner of the bar, had open-bar draft beer for everyone and just charged us a dollar a glass for our guests. It was incredibly generous of him. He's still looking for a replacement bartender, but he seems to be enjoying being behind the bar more than he was a while back. He's so friendly with everyone, and the music is so terrific, The Hive is prospering even more than ever. Sloane used some of her stash of ill-gotten money to pay the bar tab, saying she wanted to do something fun with it.

Judge Jenkins is presiding over the wedding today, and I can't help but think how different this tradition is from the puny ceremony we had in his chambers when I was sworn in as sheriff. I didn't even know who I could invite to that one, but I feel as if the entire town has shown up to celebrate with Sloane and me for this one. My heart is about ready to burst when I see the happiness on everybody's faces for us. Here I am, a grouchy nobody orphan who suddenly has an entire town feeling like my family. It's beyond wonderful.

Back when I broke off my former engagement to that cheating loser, I truly thought marriage would never be in the cards for me. I felt certain I'd never fall in love again, but little did I realize that I was never in love in the first place. It was only the hope of love and a flimsy parody of feelings. I thought my heart was crushed, but I never counted on Sloane and the emotions she made me wake up and experience. I would have had a *real* broken heart if she couldn't become mine and I hers. But wow, there's absolute ecstasy in knowing she will be mine forever in a few minutes.

I couldn't take my eyes off her the first time I met her, and I still can't today. She just gets me… and gets to me.

We made it clear that anyone who wanted to come could, including babies and children. We may end up with chaos on our hands, but it will at least be joyous chaos. I had to have a good chuckle when I saw Sammy Colfax Spencer in his baby tuxedo sitting on his granddad Mike's lap. Mike looked so proud of that kid. What a lucky child Sammy is to be surrounded by so much love. He may not be related to these grandparents by blood (he looks remarkably like Levi), but that doesn't faze anyone.

Asher was delighted when I asked him to be my best man, and Skyler was pleased as well to be a groomsman for me. Funny how they are two of the most "married" men I know who aren't actually legally married to anyone. The way they unquestioningly stepped up and helped out when Sloane was missing warmed my heart, but Asher was the one who kept me from losing my mind that day. He deserved the honor.

Levi and his band play a medley of instrumental wedding music as the guests find their seats, and once the crowd is settled, I take my place with Skyler and Asher. Then Levi begins to sing Ed Sheeran's "Perfect" in his beautiful, expressive voice. It's an unconventional wedding march, but it's perfect for us. Brooke makes her way up the aisle looking stunning in a teal gown, and then Juni strides toward us, equally resplendent in a gown of deep ruby red. Their bouquets are full of magnificent fall-colored flowers. Before Sloane makes her way toward me, I see Grover waiting like a good boy at the back of the house. He looks hilarious in his white collar and bowtie, but Sloane insisted he needed to match the other men in the wedding party. Once Juni is in place next to Judge Jenkins, Sloane, who is still hidden from view, gives Grover his cue, "Find Blake!" and he's off.

Grover trots up the aisle toward me with his tail wagging the whole way. As soon as he arrives, I bend down to give him a good pat and tell him to sit. Asher also bends down and unties the little cloth sack that is attached to his collar, holding the rings. Good dog that he is, he immediately settles at my feet and smiles at the crowd. He knows he did a great job.

When Levi gets to the part of the song about wanting to have children with the woman of my dreams, I look over at Juni, and she winks at me. She and Brooke are the only other people who know Sloane is pregnant, and they've been a great support system for her.

I look back down the aisle to see the woman I never knew I could love so much begin to walk toward me. Everything but her fades away. She is breathtaking in the gown the ladies designed and made for her. Sloane is also carrying colorful flowers because she didn't want all white. She wanted fun. And she said no to a veil. Instead, she has flowers in her golden hair that's been restored to its natural color. She looks like a goddess. And she's looking at me.

The ceremony must be lovely and moving because lots of people seem to be wiping their eyes. And we must be saying the right vows because suddenly the judge is declaring us husband and wife and telling us to kiss. But throughout all of it, I just keep thinking how lucky I am, and I cannot take my eyes off Sloane.

We did it. Sloane and I are married.

I have a family.

Epilogue

One year later

Sloane

Blake and I had the most wonderful time at our wedding, and one of my favorite parts was when we danced our first dance to the song Levi sang at Juni's party—the one about misunderstood new love and hopefulness. This was Blake's idea because he said when we danced to it the first time, it was the moment he knew he was falling in love with me—even though he didn't know what to do about it. *Aww.*

It crossed my mind later how I never, ever could have

gone through with my father's awful plan to marry Sal, and if I'd been hogtied and forced to stand in front of a priest—or even an Elvis impersonator—with that man, I still would not have been able to utter the words, "I do." But with Blake... I couldn't wait.

We took a fabulous honeymoon trip to Bermuda and relaxed for a week in a lovely resort, but we were both anxious to get back to Grover. Hayden took care of him for us and reported that Grover was excited to see Hap and Hazel again. For some reason, as soon as we got home, my baby bump appeared as if overnight, so I had to do some shopping. And get this... Juni reported she was also knocked up! She said she was inspired by Brooke and me, but I think her guys had a lot more to do with it.

Our babies were born just a couple of months apart, and I hope they grow up the best of friends with Sammy and with each other. Juni had an exquisite little girl with raven hair. There's not much guessing going on about which of her two men sired that little darling. They named her Amara Barry Hartz-Bellamy. It's a bit of a mouthful, but it's a pretty name.

Our son was born on St. Patrick's Day, so he came home from the hospital looking like a leprechaun in a green onesie supplied by the Sewing Bees. They keep a supply of holiday-themed baby outfits in the maternity ward for just such an occasion. Since we already had a Grover—and Blake still wanted to honor his old friend and mentor—we named our son

James. Everyone seems to have settled on calling him Jamie because James is just too formal for our sweet little man. Sometimes I think he looks like Blake, and other times, I think he looks like the baby photos of me that I barely remember. Maybe it's wishful thinking. I love being a mother, and Blake is beside himself. He's so proud, you'd think he was the only man who sired a baby in the history of mankind. I get it though. He never thought he'd do it, so every day that he's a father is a miracle. I can never get enough of watching my guys together. Is there anything sexier than a grown man carrying a baby?

I'm learning to juggle motherhood with teaching my classes and running the community theater. It's a challenge, but I love it all. Blake wants lots more kids, so… we'll see.

One thing that happened was rather a shock. Blake and I were fully expecting to testify at Sal's trial. The charges against him became more and more serious and complicated the longer he was incarcerated, and his lawyers were reportedly fed up with his crappy attitude and uncooperativeness. He was ultimately transferred from the Harlan County Detention Center, which is medium security, to a maximum security facility, but when word got out that he'd finally caved and ratted on some mobsters in exchange for the possibility of a lighter sentence, he got shivved by some unknown inmate. There are no suspects in his murder, and it could have just as easily been a prison guard who did it. I don't even know how to feel about any of that. I guess I'm sort of horrified and relieved at the same time.

Shortly after the wedding, I heard from my mother, and she reported that my father's business took a huge upturn when Sal got arrested. She assumes Sal was doing something that was making the business fail to begin with. I'm not ready to see her or speak to my father. Maybe I won't ever be, but at least she's not pushing me for a reconciliation, and she hasn't called again. I told her I got married, and she answered, "Did you? What does he do?" And when I told her he was a small-town sheriff in Kentucky, she said, "Oh." And that was the end of it. She doesn't know about Jamie because she hung up before I could tell her I was pregnant. I'm not even sure who gave her my number.

Being married to Blake is amazing. He's kind and listens to me like I mean something. I love cooking for him because he's always so appreciative of everything I make, and he's always hungry.

I also love living here. I've never had so many wonderful friends, and the community theater idea is working out great. Another thing I have Blake to thank for.

When I held auditions for our first variety show, it was to see what was available to schedule between the acts the various classes put on. I didn't actually turn anyone away.

My Shining Stars, who are six to nine years old, put on a stirring rendition of "Cookies for the Troll." The Drama Llamas, who are ten to thirteen, elected to do a short mystery play called "The Case of the Missing Cuckoo Clock," and my fourteen to seventeen-year-olds, the Over Actors, voted to do a comedy called "The Dog Ate My Homework." My adult actors, who are eighteen and over, ambitiously call themselves Broadway Bound. They wrote their own one-act play and called it "This Ain't Shakespeare." It was all amazing, and they had a lot of fun with their various roles. I could not have been prouder of them. There were standing ovations for everyone.

In between the short plays, we had variety acts from the community. Birdie and seven of her friends—all women of a certain age who call themselves the Hot Flashettes—performed an amazing Charleston number. They were all decked out in elaborate flapper outfits and looked gorgeous. Birdie was by far the eldest member. She's quite the woman. Also, three doctors from the local hospital formed a group called Not Quite Wayne Brady, and they did a hilarious improv scene that kept the audience in stitches. A barbershop quartet sang (mostly in tune) "By the Light of the Silvery Moon," and a band of teen boys and one girl calling themselves Stinger performed "Rhiannon" by Fleetwood Mac to tremendous applause and cheers. Those kids have a real future, if you ask me. I saw Levi and Banger talking to them after their performance.

This was our first go, and I foresee the show growing in both popularity and volume as we keep going. Stay tuned for more to come.

Honeybee Hollow *is* the best small town in America, I'm sure. The road signs don't lie.

The End

(Who am I kidding? There's always more to come).

Have you read books one and two in this series?

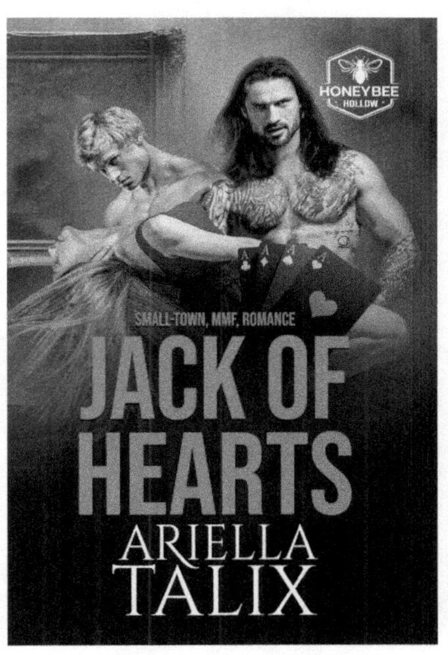

HONEYBEE HOLLOW
SMALL-TOWN, MMF, ROMANCE
JACK OF HEARTS
ARIELLA TALIX

HONEYBEE HOLLOW
SMALL-TOWN, MMF, MILITARY ROMANCE
BUDDY SYSTEM
ARIELLA TALIX

Acknowledgments

Many years ago, my brother and I camped out in the middle of nowhere in a Southern California desert with a search and rescue team. We learned from them how to track lost people both during the day and at night. It was a fascinating and potentially life-saving experience. When the guys in this book find clues along the trail toward Sloane, this was the kind of thing we were learning to find. We did not, however, have the benefit of experienced tracking dogs. Our trainers stressed safety precautions like keeping a record of what your companions are wearing, especially what kind of shoes, and recommended keeping a footprint of their shoes on a piece of paper. They also explained how lost children behave differently than adults. If you ever get the chance to learn this kind of thing, and you are a hiker or camper, I highly recommend it.

I always seem to thank the most important people at the end of this section, so this time I'll come right out and say that I love my readers, and because I've developed a loyal following, I keep writing these crazy stories. So thank you, each and every one of you who read these books. Hopefully, they offer you an escape for a while, possibly titillate you a bit, and keep you entertained. Each of these stories is a labor of love, so I hope you all keep reading and reviewing, and I hope I've touched your heart in some way that's positive.

I welcome your comments and emails: ariella@ariellatalix.com

Some other people I feel a tremendous appreciation for are those in my team of professionals. Amy Maranville of Kraken Communications is a terrific editor and is always so positive and helpful. I couldn't do this without her thoughtful input.

Mattie Davenport of Davenport Edits is amazing at her job with her proofreading, and we always managed to get into some fascinating conversation about who-knows-what. She is a marvelous professional.

My beta reader Susan has gone through some wild times since I met her years ago, and yet she is always there to offer a beautifully thought-out opinion, and I count her as one of my besties.

My wonderful cover artist Dar Albert of Wicked Smart Designs has never let me down yet. She is so talented and patient with me and always produces something I can be proud to use on my books. She is nothing short of amazing.

I started working with the ladies at Grey's Promotions a couple of books ago, so I have a heartfelt thank you to Jen DeJong and Olivia Rose who do a great job doing all the stuff I'm terrible at.

I could go on and on listing the organizers and promotors

who have put together book signings and author events, but the list would be too long, and I'd probably forget someone important. So I'm just going to say how much I appreciate all of them, especially the independent bookstore owners who put their hearts and souls into their businesses. To Rachel, Lynn, Cassie, and Brian, I wish you all success.

For some reason, I had more to discuss about this book than any of its predecessors before I could get through it. My husband had some incredibly great insight and ideas when I felt as if I was dangling off the edge of a cliff. I truly couldn't have done it without him.

And all my lovely friends have shown support and interest when I carried on and obsessed about my crazy stories. Having a network of friends, both authors and non-authors, has kept me sane when the voices in my head were either too loud or hiding away in some secret cave where I couldn't find them. Does that sound as if I'm loopy? I assure you I'm not. Of course I don't have conversations with fictitious people. I just see them acting out a movie in my head—you know, like a normal person. 😌

Anyway, thank you, everyone.

Love,

Ariella Talix

www.ariellatalix.com

You can sign up for my newsletter here:

https://landing.mailerlite.com/webforms/landing/m6f3i7

Follow me at all the obvious places:

https://www.amazon.com/stores/Ariella-Talix/author/B07MKPB8TN

https://www.facebook.com/ariella.talix.1

https://www.bookbub.com/authors/ariella-talix

https://www.instagram.com/ariellatalix/

https://www.goodreads.com/author/show/18683284.Ariella_Talix

https://x.com/AriellaTalix

$$\mathscr{B}\!ooks\ by\ Ariella\ Talix$$

Every book is a standalone story with no cliffhanger.

Each series is more fun when read in order, however. Often, characters show up again because I can't help myself.

Contemporary Romance

The Drummonds:

<u>Porter the Importer</u>

Make Believe

The Artist

Lovers in Louisville (Spin-off from The Drummonds):

Save Her

Saving Him

Savor This

Contemporary MMF Romance

The Perfect Number (Spin-off from Savor This):

The Rule of 3

The Passion of 3

Living the Fantasy:

Just Curious

Compelling Urges

Standalone:

Group Hug

Honeybee Hollow Series:

Jack of Hearts MMF novella—a spin-off from Group Hug

Buddy System Small-town, MMF, Military romance

Everybody Knows Small-town MF Romance

<u>Historical MMF Romance</u>

Hearts of Gold:

The Golden Rush

<u>Fiddle and Fire</u>

Casting Vows

<u>Anthologies</u>

Double Down on Love (*Jack of Hearts*) with the Kentuckiana Romance Writers

The Drummonds

Lovers in Louisville

The Perfect Number

Living the Fantasy